It couldn't be.

Terrance McCall. The breath in her throat caught. For one frightening second, it was as if all the carefully reconstructed pieces of her once-shattered world—the pieces she had worked so hard to put together after Terrance had vanished from her life—threatened to crack apart again.

"Alix, you look like you've seen a ghost. Do you know him?" her colleague asked.

"Yes," she replied quietly, her mouth dry, her palms damp. "I know him."

A ghost. It was a good way to describe Terrance. He was a ghost from her past. How many times had she wondered if he was dead? Had been convinced of it? Because if he were alive, she was certain he would have tried to explain how he could have gone from loving her to disappearing into some black hole, forever out of sight.

Here he was, older, handsomer, looking for all the world as if he'd just been away on an extended vacation.

And he was smiling.

Damn him to hell.

BOOK FAIR WINNIPEG, INC.
366 Portage Avenue, Wpg.
SELL – TRADE – BUY
Phone (204) 944-1630

Dear Reader,

As the year winds to a close, I hope you'll let Silhouette Intimate Moments bring some excitement to your holiday season. You certainly won't want to miss the latest of THE OKLAHOMA ALL-GIRL BRANDS, Maggie Shayne's *Secrets and Lies.* Think it would be fun to be queen for a day? Not for Melusine Brand, who has to impersonate a missing "princess" and evade a pack of trained killers, all the while pretending to be passionately married to the one man she can't stand—and can't help loving.

Join Justine Davis for the finale of our ROMANCING THE CROWN continuity, *The Prince's Wedding,* as the heir to the Montebellan throne takes a cowgirl—and their baby— home to meet the royal family. You'll also want to read the latest entries in two ongoing miniseries: Marie Ferrarella's *Undercover M.D.*, part of THE BACHELORS OF BLAIR MEMORIAL, and Sara Orwig's *One Tough Cowboy,* which brings STALLION PASS over from Silhouette Desire. We've also got two dynamite stand-alones: Lyn Stone's *In Harm's Way* and Jill Shalvis's *Serving Up Trouble.* In other words, you'll want all six of this month's offerings— and you'll also want to come back next month, when Silhouette Intimate Moments continues the tradition of providing you with six of the best and most exciting contemporary romances money can buy.

Happy holidays!

Leslie J. Wainger
Executive Senior Editor

Please address questions and book requests to:
Silhouette Reader Service
U.S.: 3010 Walden Ave., P.O. Box 1325, Buffalo, NY 14269
Canadian: P.O. Box 609, Fort Erie, Ont. L2A 5X3

Undercover M.D.
MARIE FERRARELLA

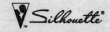

INTIMATE MOMENTS™

Published by Silhouette Books

America's Publisher of Contemporary Romance

If you purchased this book without a cover you should be aware
that this book is stolen property. It was reported as "unsold and
destroyed" to the publisher, and neither the author nor the
publisher has received any payment for this "stripped book."

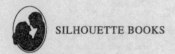 SILHOUETTE BOOKS

ISBN 0-373-27261-8

UNDERCOVER M.D.

Copyright © 2002 by Marie Rydzynski-Ferrarella

All rights reserved. Except for use in any review, the reproduction
or utilization of this work in whole or in part in any form by any
electronic, mechanical or other means, now known or hereafter
invented, including xerography, photocopying and recording, or in
any information storage or retrieval system, is forbidden without
the written permission of the editorial office, Silhouette Books,
300 East 42nd Street, New York, NY 10017 U.S.A.

All characters in this book have no existence outside the imagination of
the author and have no relation whatsoever to anyone bearing the same
name or names. They are not even distantly inspired by any individual
known or unknown to the author, and all incidents are pure invention.

This edition published by arrangement with Harlequin Books S.A.

® and TM are trademarks of Harlequin Books S.A., used under license.
Trademarks indicated with ® are registered in the United States Patent
and Trademark Office, the Canadian Trade Marks Office and in other
countries.

Visit Silhouette at www.eHarlequin.com

Printed in U.S.A.

Books by Marie Ferrarella in Miniseries

MARIE FERRARELLA

earned a master's degree in Shakespearean comedy, and, perhaps as a result, her writing is distinguished by humor and natural dialogue. This RITA® Award-winning author's goal is to entertain and to make people laugh and feel good. She has written over one hundred books for Silhouette, some under the name Marie Nicole. Her romances are beloved by fans worldwide and have been translated into Spanish, Italian, German, Russian, Polish, Japanese and Korean.

To
Sherry and Rick Newcomb,
with affection

Chapter 1

She didn't make a sound.

Even so, she felt as if her whole body had just been turned inside out and twisted. Hard.

She pressed her lips together. A silent scream filled her.

One moment, Alix DuCane was sitting in the third floor conference room, trying not to nod off as the combination of lack of air and Blair Memorial's chief of staff giving his weekly "informal" talk conspired to put her to sleep. The next, adrenaline was charging through her body like an F15 Tomcat the split second before it broke through the sound barrier.

And all because of the name that Dr. Beauchamp

had just uttered. The name of the newest addition
to the hospital's pediatric ward. Dr. Terrance
McCall.

It couldn't be.

The words vibrated within her chest.

It *couldn't* be.

Almost afraid to look, unconsciously holding her
breath, Alix shifted her eyes to the right as she detected movement from that side of the room.

It couldn't be, but it was.

Terrance.

Terry.

Oh God.

The breath in her throat caught there like a solid,
immovable lump. She felt as if she was choking.
For one frightening second, it was as if all the carefully reconstructed pieces of her once-shattered
world threatened to crack apart again. The pieces
she had worked so hard to put together after Terrance had vanished from her life, leaving her with
haunting questions and a heart that ached so badly
she was certain it would literally break.

"Alix, you okay?"

The whispered question came from her right,
from Reese Bendenetti. The surgeon leaned forward
as if to get a better look at her face.

Reese was as close a friend as she had at Blair.
She appreciated his concern, but this was something
she couldn't share. Not yet.

Very carefully she took in a deep breath, trying not to appear as stunned, as upset as she was.

"Yes, I'm okay. Thanks for asking." The quip lacked her usual verve. She hoped he wouldn't notice. The last thing she wanted right now were more questions.

Reese looked from Alix's face to the man who had come up to join Beauchamp at the podium. Blair's newest physician was tall, blond and good-looking in a rugged sort of way.

"You look like you've seen a ghost. Do you know him?"

"Yes," she replied quietly, her mouth dry, her palms damp. "I know him."

A ghost. It was a good way to describe Terrance, she thought. He was a ghost. A ghost from her past. Literally.

How many times had she wondered if he was dead? Had been convinced of it? Because if he were alive, she was certain Terrance would have gotten in touch with her, if only just once. He would have tried to explain how he could have gone from loving her, from being the center of her universe, to disappearing into some black hole, forever out of sight.

Wouldn't he have at least tried?

Yet here he was, older, handsomer, looking for all the world as if he'd just been away on a long, extended vacation.

He was smiling.

Damn him to hell.

She felt Reese shifting beside her. "You want to go out for some air?" he prodded, his voice low as Beauchamp went on talking.

Alix had known Reese for five years, and they had been there for each other, through good times and bad. He knew her as well as anyone. In all that time, she knew he'd never seen her like this. Not even when Jeff, her husband of two years, had been killed in that boating accident.

Reese could no doubt see that the man at the front of the room had left one hell of a footprint on the beach of her life.

As if set on delayed reaction, Alix waved away his suggestion, never taking her eyes off the front of the room. Off Terrance.

"I'm okay," she declared in a whisper that was a little too fierce to be true.

She wasn't okay. But she was a survivor and she would be. Even now, she tried to tell herself, the shock of seeing Terrance after all these years was abating.

Her heart rate was returning to normal.

Alix took another deep breath and let it out slowly as she forced a smile to her lips. She turned to look at Reese. She could feel the waves of his concern washing over her. It helped. Some.

"Really," she added with what she prayed was a convincing note.

Alix didn't want to admit to anything being wrong. She was incredibly independent and incredibly proud. Any show of weakness was inexcusable. She prided herself on being there for people, not vice versa.

Resigned, he nodded. "Okay, but I'm here if you want to talk."

Just as she had always been for him, Alix thought fondly. Fighting to rally and regain control over her emotions, she placed her hand over his and gave it an affectionate squeeze.

"Ditto."

Reese shook his head. "I'm not the one who just turned whiter than fresh snow at Big Bear."

And he wasn't the one who had lost his heart, utterly and completely, to the man at the front of the room, she thought. A wave of bitterness struggled to take hold of her.

Terrance McCall had been her first love, her truest love, in the days when she believed that love made you invincible and that happy endings existed beyond the pages of fairy-tale books.

What are you doing here, Terrance? After all this time, what the hell are you doing here?

Willing herself into an almost coma-like state, Alix stared straight ahead and tried to listen to what was being said. Words kept bouncing off her ears, refusing to enter or register.

Dr. Clarence Beauchamp, whose skills as a surgeon, luckily for his patients, far surpassed his oratory abilities, was still meandering his way through the introduction.

"...and Boston General's loss, of course, is Blair Memorial's gain."

The tall, portly man addressed the clichéd observation to both the young doctor standing beside him and the audience being held captive before him. Beauchamp's small lips struggled to widen into the smile that was always larger than he was actually capable of accommodating.

"Of course, we show no favoritism here at Blair. All created equal and that sort of thing." His clear blue eyes sparkled at what he must have deemed a display of wit. "Which means in your case, Dr. McCall, that you will be treated like a cross between a god-like healer and a fledgling intern. A situation," he hastened to add in case he was ruffling the pediatrician's feathers, "if your record is any indication, that will change quickly, I'm sure."

"However, for the time being you are going to need someone to show you the ropes, so to speak." Dr. Beauchamp looked pointedly around the sea of faces before him. "Someone in your department, of course. To that end, I have reviewed all the likely candidates and decided that your best bet...and ours—" he beamed again, his thin lips straining, all but disappearing into his smile "—is Dr. Alix DuCane."

Surprise speared through Terrance.

He managed to retain the easy smile on his lips. But that had come from years of training. Years of knowing that one false, unguarded moment could cost him not only the success of the operation he was involved in, but perhaps even his very life. Or worse, the lives of others depending on him.

Alix DuCane? Here?

"Alix is one of the finest young physicians on the staff," Beauchamp was saying. "No small compliment, considering that Blair Memorial was voted one of the finest hospitals not just in Southern California, but in the entire country. But you undoubtedly already know that, or you wouldn't have chosen to transfer here in the first place. Am I right, Dr. McCall?"

"Absolutely," Terrance agreed readily.

Beauchamp's voice droned on like so much well-intended noise in the background as Terrance scanned the small, crowded room and the occupants who sat almost shoulder to shoulder in the twelve rows of chairs arranged before the podium.

Accustomed to zeroing in on his target with skilled precision, Terrance found Alix in less than two beats of his admittedly agitated heart.

For a split second everything around him froze as he looked at her.

She was sitting beside a dark, good-looking man.

From his vantage point, Terrance could see her hand was covering the man's.

Friend?

Lover?

Once, he'd been both of those to her and more. So much more.

But that was in the past, Terrance reminded himself sternly, and this was the present. A present where he couldn't afford to allow his emotions to get in the way of things…the way he had once allowed his emotions to bring him into this chosen profession of his. A profession that had forced him to turn his back on everything and everyone else who had been important before.

A profession that had forced him to turn his back on Alix.

She looked pale. Shock. Small wonder if it was in response to seeing him. He felt the same way about seeing her. It was only his survival instincts that prevented him from showing it.

Even pale seemed to suit her, Terrance couldn't help thinking.

God, was it possible that Alix had grown even more heart-stoppingly gorgeous than when he had left? It appeared that the wildflower had bloomed into an exquisite orchid.

Whose life did she adorn?

Not your concern, he told himself. He'd given up the right to know, when he'd left town.

When he'd left her.

With effort Terrance roused himself, forcing his mind back to the droning voice beside him and the man who was trying his level best to make the transition easier for him.

If Beauchamp only knew....

But he didn't. A great many people had gone through a great deal of pain to ensure that. Beauchamp, along with the others, was going to be kept in the dark until the operation was over. With any luck, that would be soon.

Beauchamp took a deep breath as he ended his narrative. "Is there anything you'd like to say or add, Dr. McCall?"

Yes, Terrance thought, there was something he'd like to say. But not to the crowd of physicians looking at him. Not even to Alix. His words would have been directed to his immediate superior, uttered in quiet, steely tones and demanding to know why someone hadn't thought to let him know that he was going to be coming in contact with a vital portion of his past. That he was going to be coming in contact with the only woman he had ever loved.

Because no one knew, that's why, he reminded himself. He'd left his past behind the day he'd walked away. Still, he wished that he'd somehow been forewarned, had thought to go over the hospital roster before he'd walked through Blair's doors.

Too late now.

He could only make the best of the situation and hope that damage control would do the rest.

Terrance's mouth curved in an easy smile that gave absolutely no indication of the inner turmoil he was attempting to quell.

He leaned over the small, unnecessary microphone that Beauchamp had insisted on using. "Just that I hope to live up to the standards that the name of Blair Memorial Hospital has come to represent."

Like a proud father receiving a compliment about his favorite child, Beauchamp beamed.

"I'm sure you will, my boy." The chief of staff laid a paternal hand on Terrance's shoulder. "I'm sure you will." His eyes swept over the room and its occupants. "Well, that's it, ladies and gentlemen, meeting's adjourned. Go back to saving lives and being miracle workers."

Beauchamp chuckled at his trademark closing line. Then he raised his voice to be heard above the mounting din. "Alix, would you mind joining us?" He beckoned her forward.

Reese looked at her pointedly as he rose. "Call me," he told her firmly. "Night or day."

As if she would intrude on his life now that he was a married man. "London might have something to say about that," she reminded him.

At the mention of his wife's name, Reese grinned. Married just three months and he'd perpetually been in this state of grace that caused him to laugh to himself at unexpected, sporadic moments. As if he'd no idea that a person could feel this good and not be dreaming.

"Yes, 'Come on over,' if I know her."

Alix merely nodded. He was probably right. The daughter of the ambassador to Spain had captured her best friend's heart the instant she'd been wheeled into the emergency room last year. She was a warm, vibrant woman who had a great ability to empathize and give comfort. The two firmly deserved each other.

And what do you deserve? Alix thought as she approached the front of the room, her eyes fixed on Beauchamp and not Terrance. Certainly not to have my heart whacked around like a giant Ping-Pong ball at some phantom gaming table.

I'm over you, Terrance. I'm over you.

She silently chanted the refrain over and over again in her mind like a life-giving mantra as her steps brought her closer to the two men.

She wished she'd called in sick today. Played hooky and stayed home with her daughter. But that would have meant that Norma would have found out. The very woman who now baby-sat her child had once baby-sat her, as well. And if Norma knew something, it was only a matter of time before her father found out as well. The woman had been his housekeeper for forty years.

Daniel DuCane wouldn't have said anything to
her about her lapse, but she knew he would have
been disappointed that she would flaunt the princi-
ples to which he had dedicated his life all these
years. After all, it was because her father was a doctor that she had become one, too.

"Dr. Terrance McCall," Beauchamp gestured
from Terrance to Alix as he made the formal introduction, "This is Dr. Alix DuCane, and any compliment I could give her wouldn't be nearly
enough."

"No, it wouldn't be," Terrance agreed, his voice
a cross between being amiably impersonal and in-
timately warm—a trick, Alix felt, that only he could
pull off.

It was time to turn the herd before it stampeded
out of control and ran through the town, trampling
the citizens, Alix thought. She turned toward her
superior, ignoring Terrance.

"Dr. Beauchamp, I really don't think I'm the best
one for this assignment."

"Did I mention that she was also modest?"
Beauchamp asked Terrance. "Dedicated, skilled,
modest, don't know how we got so lucky. Nonsense, Dr. DuCane, you are most definitely the best
one for the assignment. Besides, if only half of what
I was told is correct, Dr. McCall won't require much
hand holding." The older man, a grandfather five

times over, chuckled to himself. "At least, not during official hours."

Once the words were uttered, Beauchamp must have realized the way they could be construed. His eyes slid over Alix's face nervously as if to see whether he had gone too far in his comment.

Alix knew the man meant no offense. Clarence Beauchamp wasn't capable of making any lascivious comments. He was like everyone's overly friendly, slightly addle-brained favorite uncle. Unlike his operating methods, the humor he subscribed to resided decades in the past where innocent comments were just that and carried no veiled meanings or hidden agendas. The hospital's mandatory P.C. training had taught the older man to be cautious, but that usually kicked in only after he had said something that was jarringly out of sync with the times.

Alix had her mind on something more important than imagined incorrect statements. Survival. "I've got a full load, Dr. Beauchamp."

"And you handle it beautifully," he readily testified.

Alix tried again. "I'm on E.R. rotation this morning."

If she'd hoped to deter the chief of staff, it backfired badly.

Beauchamp clapped his hands together. "Perfect." He turned to Terrance. "This'll be your trial by fire, so to speak. Can't ask for anything better than that. You'll be hurdled into the thick of our operation here. Blair prides itself on its outstanding emergency room facilities.

"Of course," the chief of staff philosophized, "Murphy's law being what it is, the E.R.'ll probably be deadly dull and quiet this morning."

Hardly that, Terrance thought, doing his best not to look at Alix as if he'd known her beyond these past five minutes. Trying not to look at her as if he knew every inch of her smooth, supple body and as if the memory of that body hadn't haunted his days and nights in vivid detail.

Pushing the past into the small, steely box where it belonged and mentally slamming the lid shut, Terrance looked down at Alix and smiled. He did his best not to take note of the dark look in her eyes.

Did I do that to you, Alix? Did I take the light away? If I did, I'm sorry that I hurt you. Sorrier than you'll ever know.

"It looks like you're going to be stuck with me for a while, Dr. DuCane," he said lightly. "I'll try my best not to get in your way."

Too late, Alix thought.

Resigned to her fate, she nodded at Beauchamp without really looking at the man. "All right, but I still think Dr. McCall would be better off with someone else. I've never been a very good teacher."

"We teach by example, Dr. DuCane, and quite

truthfully, you set the best example of anyone I can think of,'' Beauchamp assured her.

''I guess I'd better say yes before you flatter me to death,'' Alix replied.

There was affection in her voice. Clarence Beauchamp had several failings, but the ability to make a person feel good was not one of them. Though they were very different in their approaches, and her father was by far the more superior orator, Beauchamp did in some ways remind her of Daniel DuCane.

She barely spared Terrance a glance, not trusting herself.

''Follow me,'' she instructed as she turned sharply on her heel. Shoulders squared, Alix quickly walked out of the room.

Chapter 2

"Alix, wait up."

She gave no indication of having heard him as she walked quickly to the bank of elevators. With a sigh, Terrance lengthened his stride to catch up to Alix. He caught himself paraphrasing Bogart's famous line from *Casablanca*. Of all the gin joints in all the towns in all the world, I walk into hers.

"When Dr. Beauchamp said you were to show me the ropes," he told her as they reached the elevators, "I didn't think he meant that we should be swinging from them at the time."

She didn't trust herself to look at him just yet, not when he was so close. She pressed the button for the elevator. Hard.

"Sorry, I didn't realize I was moving too fast for you. I would have thought that moving quickly was something you were accustomed to."

It was, he thought, like trying to ignore the elephant in the living room. You could only do it for so long. In this case, the sooner it was addressed, the better. "Alix, maybe we should talk."

The extent of the anger that suddenly shot up inside her took Alix by surprise. It wasn't easy to force it down. But she didn't want to start shouting here, where everyone knew her. Shouting at him and demanding to know how he could have just walked away without a backward glance.

Alix took an even breath. "And maybe we shouldn't. This is a hospital, Doctor, usually a very busy place. There isn't time to sit and reminisce about old times that really didn't exist except in the imagination of someone who was very young and very foolish."

The heart he'd learned to keep on ice twisted a little. "You."

Oh, no, no pity, Alix thought fiercely. She refused to be the object of his pity. "The operating word here is *was*. In case you don't know, Doctor, that was past tense. And we're in the present. For some people that means there is no past, there is no future, there is only now." Her voice was crisp, brittle, her look cold. "I suggest that we turn our attention to now, shall we?"

Terrance looked into her eyes just before she averted them. He'd hurt her. Until this moment he hadn't realized just how much. Somehow he'd pictured her getting over him, had ached at the thought even while he assumed it was reality. He'd convinced himself that the pain over their separation had been his alone. Now he knew better.

But this wasn't the place to make apologies, even if he could fully explain to her what he'd done and why—which he couldn't. Even a minor apology necessitated somewhere quieter than the third floor of a busy hospital at midmorning.

For now, he decided, it was best to let things slide a little longer. They could pretend they were merely two former med school students whose paths had crossed again instead of two former lovers who fate—with its twisted sense of humor—had whimsically thrown in each other's way.

"You're the boss," he told her amiably. The elevator finally arrived. Getting in, Terrance watched Alix punch the button for the first floor. She jabbed at it a little too firmly. "You've gotten more assertive since the last time I saw you."

Alix felt it was more prudent not to answer.

Terrance looked down at the hand at her side. "You've also gotten married."

The words tasted like ashes in his mouth, but what had he expected? She'd move on with her life. Time didn't stand still, except for those times when he thought of her and what could have been—if a fateful bullet hadn't snuffed out his father's life and changed the course of his.

"Yes," she replied coolly, her very tone locking him out of her life. "I did."

She saw no reason to tell him that Jeff was gone, or given him any other pertinent details of her life. She just wanted to get through the day as quickly and painlessly as possible.

But it was too late for that, she thought cynically.

The elevator doors opened again on the ground floor. Alix swept out, not bothering to see if Terrance was following her. She pointed down the long corridor.

"The E.R. is this way."

Electing to bypass the patients who were seated out front, Alix took him in through the side entrance, accessible only to the hospital personnel.

Just beyond the rear nurses' station were two long rows of hospital beds, separated by partitions or floor-to-ceiling white curtains. Here and there were rooms where the more intense exams or stopgap surgeries were performed before patients were taken to the operating rooms on either the first or third floors.

Everything was in pristine condition. Blair prided itself on keeping up-to-the-minute and new. A nonprofit hospital, it relied heavily on the local community's goodwill and philanthropic donations. Its sterling reputation afforded it both.

She gestured at the rows of beds, most of which had their curtains pulled shut, signifying occupancy. Alix glanced at the large white board to the left of the nurses' station. Names and conditions were written in orange erasable marker.

"As you can see," she told him in a clipped tone of voice she was unaccustomed to using, "we're pretty full."

She noticed that Donna and Alice, two of the day nurses, were at the desk. Both stopped working the moment Terrance came into their line of vision. Both women's eyes lit up.

Some things never changed, she thought. Terrance had always been a magnet for female attention. To his credit it had never affected him. At least, not while they'd been together.

But then, who knew, maybe that had been a lie, too. Just as his words to her had been. He'd told her he loved her. And then he'd left.

Eyes riveted to Terrance, the nurses approached them as one. Alix took pity on them. "Donna, Alice, this is Dr. Terrance McCall. He'll be joining us for a while. Dr. McCall, this is Donna Patterson and Alice Brown, two of our best."

"How long a while?" Donna, never one to be shy, wanted to know.

"Time is a relative thing," Alix couldn't help saying. "What's long to some is just a moment to others."

Though he gave no indication, Terrance knew the comment was aimed at him. He smiled at the younger of the two nurses. "I plan on settling here in Bedford."

Alice lost no time in flanking his other side. Alix had the impression of two women about to launch into a tug-of-war.

"Maybe you'll need someone to show you around," Alice offered eagerly.

He could feel Alix watching him. Terrance wasn't about to allow himself to get distracted, although socializing with either woman would have been good for his cover. But with Alix here, the intended role of a carefree doctor who doubled as a ladies' man was going to have to be rethought.

"I'm originally from Bedford," Terrance told the two women.

"Nurse!" The head nurse, Wanda Monroe, called out the single title. Both women instantly turned to answer, knowing better than to ignore the imposing woman. Wanda was fair, but she brooked no nonsense when it came to the way the E.R was run. After her husband and grandchildren, the E.R. was her baby, her pride and joy, and she wasn't about to have things go lax.

Alix glanced at Terrance as Alice hurried away beside Donna. "From what I hear, you just turned down a really good time."

Terrance paused to study Alix. Was she deliber-

ately trying to get him paired off with someone? Or
was she just baiting him? "I'm not here to have a
good time, I'm here to work."

Alix looked at him, then shook her head. His eyes
were as unfathomable now as they'd ever been.

"You're just as much of a puzzle as you ever
were. FYI, the lady who just bellowed is Wanda
Monroe, our head nurse. You'd do well to stay on
her good side, which, fortunately for us, there is a
great deal of. She's part mother hen, part martinet
and the most competent nurse I've ever known."

He looked from the light-coffee-complected
woman to Alix. "That's some testimonial."

"She deserves every syllable. C'mon, I'll introduce you to her." Not waiting for Terrance to say
anything, Alix led the way over to Wanda.

Terrance took the older woman's hand and shook
it, offering a disarming smile. Wanda, he'd noted,
had been giving him the once-over from across the
room. He wondered if he passed inspection.

Wanda returned his handshake, nodding in approval. "We can always use another set of good
hands." Wanda cocked her head, peering at his
face. "Are you wet behind the ears?"

This was a woman who didn't take lies well, he
thought. But he had a feeling that she appreciated
humor.

"Maybe a little," he allowed.

Alix narrowed her eyes as she looked at him. "I

thought Dr. Beauchamp said you had a glowing record at Boston General.''

''I'm new here,'' he pointed out.

He could always turn words around to his advantage, Alix thought.

''One E.R. is like another, more or less,'' she
heard herself saying.

She wasn't ordinarily this annoyed, this distant
and impatient, Alix thought with a touch of self-
deprecation. But the sight of Terrance after all this
time had sent her reeling. It had also sent her sense
of humor into a tailspin.

''Don't you listen to her,'' Wanda contradicted
gruffly. ''They all have their own personalities. Just
like doctors,'' she added, looking pointedly at him.
''Boston General, eh?'' When he nodded, she said,
''I hear it's a fine hospital.'' Wanda crossed her
arms before her ample chest. ''What brings you
here?''

Terrance had discovered that when confronted
with questions he couldn't answer truthfully, it was
best to keep his replies simple. That way there was
less to trip him up later.

''I needed a change,'' he told her.

''Of weather?'' Wanda asked.

Terrance smiled, managing to completely charm
her and every other women within a quarter-mile
radius. Except for Alix.

''Yes.''

He was lying, Alix thought. Something else had brought him here. She could *feel* it. But lying or not, she reminded herself, it made no difference to her. His reasons for doing things had long since stopped being any business of hers.

Changing the subject, Alix nodded at the sign-in board. "Who needs attending, Wanda?"

Wanda didn't bother looking at the chart. At any given moment she knew exactly what was going on in her E.R. and who was in which bed. She didn't think of them as patients, or even by their last names. To her they were conditions in need of curing.

"Got your choice of a bad case of stomach cramps in bed K, possible urinary track infection in bed L, some woman complaining of the worst back pains she'd ever had in bed M or—"

The electronic back doors flew open as four paramedics charged in, pushing two gurneys between them. A much-battered woman lay very still on the first, a screaming child on the second.

"Incoming," Alix announced, snapping to life. "Looks like you're on, Doctor."

Terrance wished she'd stop calling him that. She sounded so formal, so distant. He fell into step beside her, wondering if he could get used to the new Alix.

But he supposed that he had it coming to him.

He couldn't afford to dwell on the past now. This

was a bona fide emergency he had before him. Terrance prayed that the week he'd spent at the hospital in Boston was enough to refresh his memory about how to deal with whatever came his way.

"Oh, God," Alix groaned. Her eyes were focused on the second gurney, on the child who looked to be just a little older than her own daughter. "What happened?" she demanded of the closest paramedic.

"Mother's got a history of unstable mental behavior," the man with "Jerry" stitched on his uniform pocket answered. Details came spilling out as quickly as vital signs ordinarily did. "Happened at the courthouse. She was despondent over a custody hearing. Grabbed the little girl and ran up to the roof. Jumped holding the kid's hand." He saw Alix looking from one gurney to another. "She's DOA, Doc, just waiting for you to make the official call."

"And the little girl?" Alix wanted to know, raising her voice above the screaming child.

The head of the second team rattled off the small victim's vital signs. The readings could all be far better, but there was reason to hope.

"How is it she's still breathing?" Terrance marveled.

"Kid fell on top of the mother," he was told by the paramedic on the gurney's other side.

"Probably saved her life," Alix commented. She looked up. "Wanda?"

The head nurse understood her shorthand and pointed. "Room four's free."

Sliding her arms through the sterile, yellow paper gown one of the nurses was holding out for her, Alix never took her eyes off the child.

"You know the way," she told the second team. Together they hurried down the corridor.

"Hey, what about Mom?" the first paramedic wanted to know.

Alix spared the dead woman a glance. "She wasn't a mom, she was a monster." She looked at Terrance. For a moment she thought he almost appeared lost. "I'll leave the honor of calling it to you, Doctor. Welcome to Blair," she added dryly.

With that Alix hurried alongside the gurney into Room Four to do everything in her power to save the life of an innocent child whose only sin was to have the misfortune of being born to the wrong woman. Mentally she recited a prayer as the doors closed behind her.

A moment later a man came tearing in through the same electronic doors that had parted to admit the two teams with their gurneys. Frantic, he grabbed the first person he encountered, an orderly who spoke next to no English and looked terrified by the man's demeanor.

"My little girl, they just brought her in." The man looked up and down the hall. Everything blurred before him. "She's only two—"

There was barely harnessed hysteria in the man's voice. Terrance looked up from the bloodied woman on the gurney. Even if he were the most skilled doctor in the world, he could do nothing for her now.

But there was something he could do for the father.

Placing his body between the gurney and the man, he stopped the latter from plowing into it. Terrance clamped a hand on the man's shoulder. "They've taken her into the exam room."

It took a second for the words to process. "Is she…is she…?" He couldn't bring himself to utter the unutterable.

Terrance's hand remained on the man's shoulder, holding him in place. "She's alive," Terrance assured him.

"And my wife?" Utterly beside himself, the man was blind to the still figure that lay on the gurney directly behind Terrance.

Terrance noted that the man referred to the woman as his wife, not his ex-wife. There were feelings there, he judged, vividly brought out by the tragic events of the moment.

He wondered if there were doctors who got used to saying this. He knew he didn't. "I'm sorry. She didn't make it."

For a second Terrance thought the man was going to crumple before him at his feet. He seemed to get weak at the knees and sagged against Terrance as he saw the body of his wife.

"Maybe it's better this way. Maybe Jill'll finally be at peace." There were tears in his eyes as he turned them toward Terrance. "But why did she have to try to take Wendy with her? She's just a little girl, a baby." His voice hitched badly. "She's got her whole life in front of her."

It never made any sense, but Terrance tried to find an explanation for him.

"Maybe your wife thought that Wendy couldn't survive without her." That was the most common psychological profile when it came to mothers who killed their children and then themselves. It revolved around a fear that the children left behind couldn't really function in a world without the parent.

The man didn't seem to hear. Instead he began to look around frantically, heading for the first curtained bed. "Where is she? Where did they take Wendy?"

Terrance drew him away before he could frighten a patient. "To Room Four for examination."

He indicated the room Alix and the nurses had entered. The man hurried over to it. Terrance was right behind him, wondering if the man, in his grief, was going to have to be restrained. He cut him off before he had a chance to enter the room.

"They're doing all they can for her. If there's even an infinitesimal chance of saving your daughter, they will. Dr. DuCane's with her right now, and they're sending for an internal surgeon.''

At least, he assumed they were. Terrance knew he had to keep up a steady stream of conversation to distract the man. It was the best service he could offer in this situation. He knew how to treat common ailments, but what was going on behind the closed swinging doors to his right was beyond the scope of his expertise. Surgery for him meant removing pieces of glass from a cut or stitching up a simple wound.

Cushioned fall or not, the little girl they had just brought in was going to need some serious surgery—and someone who was up on what they were doing. That left him out.

Terrance thought of the lounge where patients' family members waited for the results of operations. He'd passed it on his way in this morning. ''Why don't I take you someplace where you can sit down and—''

But the man shook off the hand that Terrance placed on his arm. ''I don't want to sit. I want to be right here. Right here,'' he repeated numbly, ''in case they need me.''

Angling around Terrance, he tried to get a better look through the windowed portion of the swinging doors. There was a ring of people around the table. He could make out the small form on the gurney.

''She's so little,'' he sobbed.

"Somehow they mend quicker when they are."
Terrance knew he was mouthing every platitude he
could think of, but he needed to calm the man down.
"She's going to be all right."

He saw the head nurse he'd met only minutes ago
looking in his direction. He could tell by her expression that she'd overheard him. Wanda shook her
head. His earlier training reminded him that he was
violating a cardinal rule at the hospital: you never
made promises you couldn't keep.

But he knew how important it was to hand out
hope, to offer it at least for a moment. Because he'd
been on the other side of the operating room doors
once himself, when his father had been the one the
medical team were working over.

Small bits of precious hope, however unfounded,
had kept him functioning and sane, had enabled him
to keep his mother's spirits up. And, eventually, had
helped him cope with his father's death.

It was the least he could do for the man who
looked as if his whole world had shattered right before his eyes. The least and the most.

Down the corridor he saw Wanda waving to the
orderlies who were taking the woman's body away.
He thought of directing the man's attention to that,
then decided against it. Instead, he stayed beside the
father, whose eyes remained fixed on the activity
around his daughter's table.

"She'll be all right," Terrance repeated and
prayed that Alix wouldn't make him a liar.

Chapter 3

"Doctor, why don't you go on in there now?"

Unnoticed—a remarkable feat considering her size—Wanda had come up behind Terrance and the little girl's distraught father as they stood outside the examination room.

"I'll take care of Mr.—" Wanda paused as she looked at the man. Her eyes were filled with understanding and compassion.

"Carey," the man mumbled without seeming to be aware that he had said anything. He leaned his fisted hands against the upper portion of the exam room door, as if to somehow brace himself and help ward off the very worst.

"I'll take care of Mr. Carey," Wanda repeated,

slipping a comforting arm around his shoulders. Though the man was taller than she, he seemed vulnerable and smaller. The events of the morning had diminished him.

Wanda glanced over her shoulder toward Terrance when he made no attempt to move. She made a slight movement of her brows, narrowing them quizzically, as she led Carey away to the lounge.

Terrance had no choice. Unless he wanted to arouse the head nurse's suspicions, he had to go into the exam room. Feeling incredibly out of place, he pushed open the swinging door and entered.

The instant he did, a wall of noise and chaos reached out and grabbed him, sucking him into its midst.

Alix glanced up in his direction. There were tubes running into the little girl's mouth and attached to both her arms. The readings didn't look promising, but at least there was still activity going on.

"Nice of you to join us, Doctor," she noted coolly. Several of the nurses exchanged glances. They weren't used to Alix being anything other than warm and friendly. "Where have you been?"

"With her father." Terrance's answer was lost in the shuffle of people as behind him, another man entered the room.

"You called for a miracle worker?"

Terrance turned and saw the man who'd been sitting beside Alix in the meeting join the fray. Despite the obvious circumstances, the latter smiled warmly at her.

"You got that right," Alix said. It was beginning to look to Alix as if the little girl might need more than just one doctor to help her make it. Alix rattled off a capsulized version of what had happened. "Mother jumped from the roof of the courthouse, taking her daughter with her." It never did any good to try to distance herself from her cases. Her heart was too big to allow it, even though it cost her emotionally. "She's got all sorts of internal damage going on, but she's hanging in there. She's a fighter." Alix brushed the bangs away from the girl's forehead. "Poor little thing."

"Wendy," Terrance said. Alix looked up at him sharply. "Her father said her name's Wendy."

"Well, she certainly wasn't meant to fly, at least not without Peter Pan," Reese commented, looking toward the closest nurse. "Call up to the O.R. and tell them to get a room ready immediately, Donna. Then page Dr. Owlsey. I have a feeling I'm going to need all the help I can get here." As the nurse ran to the wall phone, Reese looked at Alix. The orderly beside him was taking the brakes off the bed, mobilizing it for the trip to the elevator. "Want to come along?"

Alix shook her head. She knew she'd be of more use down here. "I'll only get in your way. I'll stop by later to see how she's doing." She smiled at him. "I've got faith in you, Reese."

Terrance tried not to remember when that smile had been his alone to absorb. He clamped down on any extraneous feelings that threatened to seep through. Like the lady had said, the past was the past. There was no use in going there.

"Good to know," Reese quipped. He looked at Terrance as he hurried beside the bed from the exam room. "Reese Bendenetti, internal surgery."

"Nice to meet you," Terrance called after the man. Reese, the bed and the two nurses and one orderly with him disappeared around the corner.

Terrance blew out a breath, realizing that he'd been in the midst of an adrenaline rush without knowing it. Ordinarily when he experienced one there were guns involved. And usually a drug bust.

With one drama now beyond her control, Alix turned toward Terrance, annoyance etched into her expression. "Where the hell *were* you?" she demanded. Shedding the yellow gown, she shoved it into a trash basket, her eyes blazing. "You were supposed to be in there with me."

"I was."

Typical. He was playing with words. Just as he always had. "From the *beginning,* Doctor."

She was swiping at him. He figured he owed this to her. "I already told you. I was outside, comforting the father."

Alix pressed her lips together to keep back choice comments. She'd never felt so out of control, so unsettled. "We have nurses for that."

"I know," he replied quietly, refusing to be drawn into an argument. "Wanda took him over. But at the time, it seemed like the thing to do." Maybe if he complimented her, she'd back off. "Besides, you seemed to be on top of it."

She never felt on top of it. She always felt that there was a little more she could do, even as her patients were pulling through. There was always the nagging concern that something had been overlooked, that her efforts weren't enough.

But part of her success, part of the reason her patients did so well and their parents always returned to her, was that she knew how to make it seem as if she *was* on top of a situation. She knew how to make them think that she had all the answers even before the questions were formed. Knew how to make them feel confident.

She wished she could say the same for herself. It was all a ruse. She supposed that gave her something in common with magicians and actors.

"That's no excuse," she told him tersely. "You're here to assist and learn our way of doing things." She fisted her hands at her waist as she looked up at him. He was a good ten inches taller. "Or don't you think you need to?"

The fire in her eyes had him feeling nostalgic

despite the sharpness in her voice. There was a time when he would have warmed himself at that fire, rather than feel it as a threat. "I know better than to be lured into a fight with you, Alix."

She resisted the temptation to tell him to call her Dr. DuCane. She wanted no more familiarity between them than was absolutely necessary. "Oh, really? I wouldn't have thought you knew anything about me at all."

Terrance looked around for someplace more private. "Look, I—"

Whatever he had to say, she didn't want to hear it. There was nothing that could be said to whitewash what had happened six years ago.

"Why don't you make yourself useful and take the patient to Bed K?" It was not a suggestion, but an order, issued crisply. "I'll be around if you need me."

Terrance remembered how she used to say that to him when they were studying for their MCATS. She'd always been the better student. The familiar phrase brought a smile to his lips. "Just like old times."

Her eyes narrowed. "Nothing at all like old times," she informed him tersely. "Bed K," she repeated, pointing toward the general area as she walked away. "The nurse said he has projectile vomiting, so I'd stand clear if I were you."

As Alix rounded the desk at the nurse's station,

Wanda made a comment. "Seems to be sparks flying between you and that new miracle worker."

Alix punched her ID into the computer. A screen popped up, and she began a search for information she needed to treat one of the patients she'd admitted early this morning.

God, this was all she needed, hospital gossip. "No sparks, Wanda."

The woman snorted. "Didn't look that way from where I was standing."

Alix slanted a quick glance in her direction. "Then I'd say that you were obviously standing in the wrong place."

"Yes, Doctor." Wanda's tone was sing-songy and falsely deferential.

Alix looked up from the screen, flashing a contrite smile. "Sorry, Wanda. I didn't mean to snap."

"No," Wanda readily agreed, "you didn't. Need to talk?"

That was the last thing Alix wanted to do. The less said about Terrance, the better. "No."

But Wanda wasn't put off. Cocking her head, she crossed her arms before her ample chest. "I've got three kids and a passel of grandkids, Doctor D. I know when someone needs to talk."

Alix looked at her for a long moment, then sighed. "Maybe I can't."

"Now that's different," the older woman allowed. "I can understand that." She gave Alix's shoulder a maternal pat. "But don't hold it in too long, Dr. D., or you're liable to explode. And I'm not cleaning up that mess when you do." Her pseudo-serious warning faded as she studied Alix. Something was most definitely going on here. She was far too good a judge of human nature not to notice. "In case you're wondering, he seems to have a good bedside manner."

"No." Alix's fingers flew over the keyboard. "I wasn't wondering."

From the way Wanda smiled, it seemed she was willing to bet that Alix knew all about Terrance McCall's bedside manner firsthand.

"I meant with your patient's father. Just because they issue someone a stethoscope doesn't mean they know how to handle people. Sometimes the best medicine they can dispense is a dose of hope, even if there's not much available."

Alix nodded dismissively. Wanda was right. A good bedside manner was a much-underrated ability. But right now she wasn't willing to give Terrance any accolades, deserved or otherwise. Finding what she needed on the computer, she made a mental note and logged off.

"You've got my number if you change your mind," Wanda called after her.

That made two people who'd offered her a shoulder to cry on, she thought, walking away. Not that she was going to take either of them up on it. She'd cried herself out a long time ago. There were literally no tears left. Not for anything.

If there had been, she would have shed them for the little girl she'd worked on.

Since the turmoil in the E.R. had gone down a notch after Reese had taken Wendy Carey up into surgery, Alix decided that it wouldn't hurt anything to stop by the small chapel on the premises before she went on with her duties.

And maybe it would even help a little—both her and the little girl. Involuntarily her thoughts turned to Terrance's sudden reappearance. She could do with a little something extra on her side right now.

''So how's it going?''

Rounding a corner, Terrance stopped short. He'd almost walked directly into a dark-haired, cocky-looking orderly wielding a cart of empty lunch trays.

He recognized the voice even before he looked at the man. Terrance smiled wearily.

''That stint in Argentina's beginning to look better and better in comparison all the time. At least no one threw up on me in Buenos Aires.''

True to Alix's prediction, the patient in Bed K had vomited all over him. An hour and one change of clothes later, he still felt the smell of the incident clinging to him. It was a hell of a start.

Riley Sanchez, a perfect blend of an Irish mother

and a Spanish father, flashed a row of brilliantly white teeth. "But you've got to admit that the scenery's nicer here." Riley leaned in closer, lowering his voice. "Have you checked out some of the nurses?"

"We're not here to check out nurses, remember?"

"Can't help it if they walk into my line of vision." Riley's grin broadened. "I noticed that the lady doctor they assigned you to isn't exactly someone who'd stop a clock. That's one fine-looking woman."

Riley's laid-back, easygoing demeanor belied the sharp mind that lay beneath. Nothing worth noting ever got past Riley, which was what made him so good at his job. His humor made him an asset when times got tough. But right now Terrance was in no mood for any of his partner's witticisms.

Riley saw the way Terrance's jaw tightened at the mention of his guide. "Something wrong?"

He didn't feel like getting into it, certainly not here. "No."

Like a dog with a bone, Riley didn't let go. "Well, it's not right," he observed. He stopped, thinking of the man they suspected. "She's not connected to…?"

"No," Terrance said firmly, "she's not."

That much he knew. Alix couldn't and wouldn't be involved in the reason he and Riley were here.

Alix DuCane was as honest as they came, incapable of lying or anything more serious. He'd stake his life on it. Some things, no matter what, just didn't change.

Shifting, Riley studied him. "Judging by the way you just said that, you're pretty certain. It's too soon for you to have bonded with the lovely lady doctor, which means that you know her from a previous life."

Terrance took the high road and dismissed Riley's words at face value. "I'm not into reincarnation."

"Neither am I. I was talking about the life we had before we sold our souls to the agency."

"Go do a profile on someone else, Riley." The subject was closed.

Riley nodded, backing off for now. He'd worked with McCall off and on over the past six years, the last two steadily. He knew it would do no good to press Terrance, who came around according to his own timetable.

"That's what they pay me for." Riley glanced over his shoulder and saw the head nurse was looking his way. She didn't look pleased. "Time to get busy."

Terrance sighed, thinking of the afternoon that was ahead. His endless days and nights as an intern came rushing vividly back at him. "I never stopped."

"Catch you later," Riley murmured, beginning to guide the cart toward the service elevators and ultimately the kitchen located in the basement. "Don't look now, but your lady friend is walking this way."

Terrance turned in time to see Alix heading in his direction. Now what?

Alix had never been one to shirk her duty, no matter how distasteful or difficult it was. She placed dealing with Terrance in that category.

Telling herself that she was no longer the young woman she'd once been did no good. In her heart Alix sincerely doubted if she would ever be completely over Terrance McCall.

But there was absolutely no reason to let him know that.

As she drew closer, a foul odor assaulted her nose. She sniffed, then realized that the smell was coming from the same vicinity as Terrance.

"Is that coming from you?"

He nodded. "Patient in Bed K threw up on me, just like you predicted." He was wearing a lab coat that was entirely too snug in the shoulders and had had to change his shirt and pants. "One of the residents lent me his clothes."

Alix nodded. "That would explain the scrubs."

She'd forgotten how good he looked in the attire. And how much it had once turned her on. This time, however, he looked like someone who'd gotten caught in the rain and had his clothes shrink. The cuffs of his pants exposed a section of dark sock.

"Rafferty?" she guessed, referring to one of the residents on the floor.

He glanced down to see if the man's name was written on the lab coat. It wasn't. Terrance looked at her, surprised. "How did you know?"

"Process of elimination. He's shorter than you are. Adam Hathaway's about the same height," she judged. "They're the only two doctors in the E.R. right now." The odor was getting to her. She wrinkled her nose. "I'd suggest you take a shower."

"Can't." When she looked at him quizzically, he leaned over and whispered, "In case you haven't heard, the head doctor's pretty strict. If I leave my post for more than a minute, she'll have my head."

Alix wasn't amused. She looked at him pointedly, making herself, she hoped, perfectly clear. "The head doctor doesn't want your head, Doctor. Or any other part of you, either."

Maybe he'd overstepped his boundaries. Feelings for her or not, the woman was married and he had his rules. She had nothing to worry about from him. "Duly noted. Just so I'm clear on this, are you telling me to take a shower?"

Alix nodded. "For the good of the hospital," she affirmed.

He wasn't about to argue the point. Terrance

couldn't help wondering how many people he'd of-
fended in the last hour. "Where would I—"

"There's a facility directly behind the doctors'
lounge. Slightly bigger than a bread box, but if
you're not planning to do any acrobatics while
showering, it'll do the trick."

Funny she should mention that. It brought back
to mind the showers they'd taken together, fitting
against each other in a tiny stall. Sometimes they
would even remember to turn the water on.

"Thanks. And Alix—"

She knew that tone, that pause. He was going to
say something she was better off not hearing—even
though part of her hungered to.

But that was her weakness, and she would deal
with it. The way she'd always dealt with everything
else that life had thrown her way. She'd learned to
savor the good moments, trusting the memory of
them to see her through, like a bridge to the next
good moment.

"Go take your shower," she ordered. With that,
she turned on her heel and walked away.

Terrance raised his voice. "It's good to see you
again," he called after her.

Without bothering to turn around, Alix waved her
hand at him, dismissing the words.

Dismissing him.

Telling himself he didn't feel stung, Terrance
turned away. Like he'd just told Riley, they weren't

here to fraternize or enjoy the "scenery," they were here to bring the operation to a successful close.

On that thought he began to walk quickly to the doctors' lounge.

Just behind him, he heard the rear emergency room doors opening and the sound of a gurney being hurried in. Turning around, he could see the blood even from where he stood.

The shower was going to have to wait.

Terrance broke into a run. He caught Alix's expression out of the corner of her eye as she approached from another direction. He wouldn't have been able to say why the unguarded look of approval pleased him the way it did, but it did.

Chapter 4

Terrance frowned slightly as he set down his tray on the table and slid into the corner booth in the hospital cafeteria. The vantage point allowed him a full view of the area just beyond the entrance.

Things were going slower than he wanted. He'd been at Blair Memorial for almost a week and had learned nothing.

No, that wasn't strictly true, he amended silently. He might not have gotten anywhere in his investigation, but he had learned that his first career choice did hold an attraction for him, even after a self-imposed absence of six years.

He'd learned, too, that the woman who had been so important to him while he was studying to be a doctor most definitely still held an attraction for him. Time had done nothing to diminish that. But then, he hadn't left her because he'd lost interest in her the way he had with medicine. Alix hadn't been the reason he'd gone numb inside, becoming all but clinically dead yet still somehow going through the motions. Medicine had done that. Or rather, medicine's failure had done that to him.

The inability of medicine to save his father's life after Jake McCall had been shot during a DEA stakeout had shaken the very foundations of Terrance's world, had made him question everything that he felt he was about.

The moment his father had taken his last breath, medicine had ceased to hold any allure for Terrance. He found he had to get away, to think, to somehow try to reinvent himself. That meant leaving his old life behind.

That meant leaving Alix behind, as well, because she deserved someone who was whole—not him. She deserved someone who could love her, and he no longer knew if he was capable of the kind of love she needed.

So he'd left Bedford and Alix and refused to look back. Left her without saying a word. It was the coward's way out, the only time he'd taken it, but it was the only way he could have walked away.

Now he wasn't so sure that he had done the right thing.

Too late for second thoughts now, McCall. She's married to someone else.

That meant that he'd lost the right to let that bother him, certainly lost the right to try to reaffirm his position in her life. Even if he were so inclined, which he wasn't.

He was what time and circumstances had forced him to become. A loner. In his chosen profession, that was viewed as an asset. No wife to worry about, no family to slip into his thoughts at the wrong moments, taking his edge off, blurring his focus. The best agents were the ones who were married to the job, not to a flesh-and-blood person.

He knew all that, and yet…

And yet nothing, Terrance thought. He was here to try to get close to William Harris, the grandson of the founder of this hospital, not to conjure up regrets and fantasize over what might have been.

He was familiar with the hospital, the first in Bedford. Known then as Harris Memorial, the eight-story, multiwinged edifice had only recently been renamed Blair Memorial in honor of the woman who had bequeathed her entire fortune to the hospital upon her death.

Terrance smiled to himself. For a fifty-million-dollar bequest, he would have allowed himself to be renamed Shoe.

"Mind if I join you?"

Terrance roused himself from his thoughts.

You're not doing your job, he admonished himself silently. Looking up, he saw the chief of staff standing beside his table, holding a tray in his hands. It contained a single plate of deep-dish apple pie.

Terrance indicated the empty seat opposite him. "Please." He tried not to notice that easing his considerable bulk onto the booth bench took a bit of maneuvering for Beauchamp.

The older man slid his plate from his tray onto the table and smiled a little self-consciously. He rested the tray against the side of his seat, out of the way.

Beauchamp picked up a fork with enthusiasm. "Yes, just dessert. I really set a poor example, I'm afraid." He sank the fork into his serving. A look of anticipation entered his eyes. "I know I should be eating better. 'Physician, heal thyself,' and all that, but quite honestly, come midafternoon all I want to do is eat something sweet." The first mouthful had him sighing with pure contentment and pleasure.

Terrance grinned at the unabashed display. "I wasn't looking at your choice, Dr. Beauchamp. I was just surprised to see you here. I didn't think you frequented the cafeteria."

"Oh there's a small dining hall across the way reserved for doctors only, but I find I like getting down in the trenches with everyone else. We all put our pants on the same way," he said lightly. Another forkful disappeared into his mouth before he asked, "So tell me, how is it going? Fitting in?"

The pie was disappearing at an impressive rate, yet the man seemed to be slowly savoring every bite. Terrance marveled, watching him. "I'd like to think so."

"I've been hearing good things about you from the staff," Beauchamp informed him. "You seem to have gotten on Wanda's good side." He nodded his whole-hearted approval. "Always a good thing. She can be a formidable adversary if she doesn't like you."

Though no pushover, the head nurse had been nothing but amiable to him. She made him think of a mother hen. "I can't see Wanda actually giving anyone any grief. She seems fair enough."

"Oh, she is, she is," Beauchamp agreed enthusiastically, then confided in a lower voice, "But she doesn't like people who think they know it all." The older man shook his head. "She and young Harris have never gotten along, I'm sorry to say. But then, he does seem to have a problem."

Beauchamp suddenly looked startled, as if he'd just heard his own pronouncement. "Don't get me wrong," he said quickly, launching into damage-control mode. "William Harris is a good doctor and all that, it's just that—" It wasn't in him to lie. "Well, he could stand to have his ego taken down a notch or two. But that's what comes of having everything handed to you, I suppose. A little hard work is good for everyone.''

Terrance estimated that he probably knew far more about William Harris than the man sitting opposite him. There was a two-inch-thick file on the man on his desk back at the agency. But it was one thing to have information before you and another entirely to listen to it being rendered firsthand. Sometimes, that kind of insight was just the thing to break an investigation wide open.

He looked at Beauchamp innocently. ''If you feel that way, why keep him on?''

''Oh, it wouldn't do to release the grandson of the founder of the hospital. The money might be coming from other sources these days, but the waves something like that might generate—'' Beauchamp shook his head, finishing his statement silently as he retreated into another bite of his pie. ''Well, it just wouldn't do, that's all.'' He peered at Terrance, wanting to change the subject. ''Getting along well with Dr. DuCane?''

Terrance wondered if he was actually being grilled a little. The man had an innocent face, but Terrance was willing to bet Beauchamp wasn't as guileless as he seemed. ''Yes.''

''She's a wonderful woman. And dedicated.'' Beauchamp nodded as he recalled past events. ''Refused to take any time off after that terrible accident.

She was in the very next week, acting as if nothing had happened. She's a strong, strong woman.''

Terrance looked at him. He'd deliberately refrained from looking into Alix's past, feeling as if he were taking advantage of his position and invading her privacy. But now that Beauchamp had drawn back this curtain to reveal her life, he had to know. "What terrible accident?"

"Why, the one that took her husband, Jeff," Beauchamp said, then seemed to realize Terrance's confusion. "Jeffrey Caldwell. He was on staff here, too. Just like Dr. DuCane not to mention anything. For a bright, sunny woman, she doesn't talk about her own life very much. Me," he confided, "I tend toward ear bending, but Dr. DuCane is more concerned with listening than talking—other than to bolster spirits, of course. They don't make them like her anymore," he said wistfully.

No, Terrance thought, they didn't. But then, he already knew that. He pressed for more information. "How long has her husband been dead?"

"Jeff? Let me see." Beauchamp paused as he made a few mental calculations. "It's been almost two years—no, wait," he corrected himself, "a little more than that. Yes, two years ago in April." His head bobbed up and down in confirmation. "It was a boating accident. One of those freak things you don't believe is happening until it's over."

"Was she there?" Terrance couldn't think of

anything worse than Alix witnessing her husband's death.

"No, she was home with her little girl," Beauchamp recalled. "Julie had a cold." Intent on the last of his pie, he didn't see the look that suddenly came into Terrance's eyes.

Julie. She'd named her daughter Julie. Was it a coincidence or had she deliberately named the child after his late mother? The two women had gotten close when he'd been seeing Alix. He'd always had the suspicion that it was because Alix was hungry for a mother's affection. Her own mother had died when she was very young.

"I didn't know she had a little girl," he said quietly to the other man.

"Now *that* I'm surprised about. Dr. DuCane does like to show off pictures of her daughter." Beauchamp pushed the empty plate away and looked at Terrance, studying the younger man. "Are you two getting along?"

"Yes," Terrance assured him. "We're getting along." As well as could be expected, he thought. "I have no complaints."

Beauchamp seemed pleased. "Good, good. Let me know if there's anything I can help you out with."

You already have, Terrance thought. But now it was time to get down to the crux of why he was here in the first place. "I was just wondering, have I seen this Dr. Harris you mentioned?"

Beauchamp shook his head. "Ordinarily, Dr. Harris would be on now, but he's taken a few days off. Something about needing to catch a breather." Terrance thought he detected a note of disapproval in the jovial man's voice. "Does most of his breathing in Las Vegas, I hear. At the blackjack tables." Beauchamp banished the slight purse of his lips. "Never liked to gamble myself. I go with sure things. Like this hospital," Beauchamp said with no small pride. He seemed to make it his business to know the comings and goings of all the doctors on staff. "To answer your question, though, Harris should be back tomorrow." He cocked his head, curious. "Why?"

Terrance shrugged carelessly. "Just wondering what the man who ruffles Wanda's feathers looked like."

"Oh, he ruffles more feathers than just Wanda's, but like I said, good will is worth a great deal and everyone likes the man's father." The senior Harris had preceded Beauchamp as chief of staff and was now chairman of Blair's board of trustees. "Arthur Harris is one of the most respected doctors in the West."

Terrance merely nodded, as if all this was news to him. He couldn't help wondering what the man sitting opposite him would say if he knew Terrance's real purpose for being here.

Terrance glanced at his watch. "I'd better get going." He rose, picking up his tray. "I don't want to get on Dr. DuCane's bad side."

Beauchamp laughed. "Good thinking."

Terrance's afternoon was taken up by a man who came in complaining of chest pains which turned out to be a case of indigestion. He'd also had two cases of otitis media, the latter coming via a set of twins. It wasn't until almost three o'clock before Terrance had a chance to catch up with Alix.

"Why did you tell me you were married?"

Alix made a notation on the chart of a girl who'd come in with an ectopic pregnancy. They'd had to rush her into surgery.

She didn't bother looking up. "Because I am," she replied mildly.

He knew he should drop it, that he was only getting in deeper, but the fact that she'd lied to him, or at least misled him, bothered him. It just wasn't like her. "Doesn't being married require that there be two *living* people in the union?"

She closed the chart and glared at him. "Who told you?"

He leaned against the side of the desk. "Dr. Beauchamp likes to socialize over apple pie."

She laughed shortly, but couldn't muster any anger toward the chief of staff.

"Dr. Beauchamp likes to socialize over anything." Her smile faded as she looked at Terrance. "But to answer your presumptuous question, as far as I'm concerned, I *am* married. I didn't divorce Jeff, he died on me."

"Technically," Terrance said, "that makes you a widow."

The word made her think of dark clothes and sad-eyed women who were old years before their time. "I don't like the term."

It'd been a week, he thought. Some of the barriers should have broken down a little. "Okay, how does *available* sound?"

Her eyes narrowed and darkened. Like her expression. "Like a lie. I'm not," she said with finality. The last thing she wanted was to leave herself open to more pain. "My heart has seen enough action to last a lifetime, Doctor. It's tired. It doesn't need to buy another ticket to a roller-coaster ride."

She was putting him on notice, Terrance thought. Try as he might, he couldn't blame her. He wished he could, but he couldn't. But there was something else he could blame her for. "You didn't tell me about your daughter, either."

He had no right to her private life. Not anymore. "Correct me if I'm wrong, but I was told to show you the ropes at the hospital. I was not told to lay my life bare to you."

For a second he lost his way. She always did have a knack of getting to him, even when he pretended that she didn't. "We have a history."

Oh, no, he wasn't going to use that against her, to wield it to his advantage. That was emotional blackmail. Alix raised her chin defiantly.

"Right, and by definition *history* means something that happened in the past. We have a past, Terrance," she agreed tersely. "Under no circumstances do we have a future, and as soon as Dr. Beauchamp allows you to fly solo, we won't even have a present."

She'd blocked off every path but one. He availed himself of it. "All right, I have some questions about the hospital."

Alix bit back a groan and braced herself. "Go ahead."

But Terrance shook his head. "I want to ask them over coffee."

He didn't have any questions, she thought, he was just trying to get her alone. "Why?"

Terrance shrugged innocently. "I think better with caffeine flowing through my veins."

He hadn't cared for coffee when she'd known him. Alix wondered what else there was about him that she didn't know, then told herself that it didn't matter. The man he was now didn't matter. And the man she'd once loved was gone. He'd walked out on her.

She had to remember that.

Playing along, she said, "There's a pot in the doctor's lounge."

She'd always been a good chess player, Terrance recalled. "I was thinking of the small outdoor café across the street."

"I wasn't." She gave him her terms. "Doctors' lounge or nothing."

The look in her eyes told him she meant it. "Doctors' lounge."

"Sorry, Alix, some numbskull broke the coffeepot." Dr. Holly Xavier held up the cracked pot to back up her statement uttered in disgust. "That new orderly, Sanchez, volunteered to go buy a new one on his break."

Good old Riley, always making points, Terrance thought.

Alix sighed as she looked at the coffeepot.

"Outdoor café?" Terrance prodded.

She turned around to face him. "Hospital cafeteria," she countered.

At least in the hospital cafeteria the cocooning din would keep her safe. She knew that if they went anywhere quieter, the sound of his voice was liable to rouse things within her, to unlock doors she'd closed and permanently boarded up.

There was a time when he could almost read her thoughts. He had a little insight into them now. Terrance looked at her pointedly. "Why are you afraid of being alone with me?"

Alix stiffened, her eyes took on fire. "I am not afraid." She looked at her watch. They only had twenty minutes. "And the minutes of our break are slipping away."

He knew when to give an inch in hopes of eventually gaining a mile. Terrance spread his hands magnanimously. "Cafeteria it is."

Turning on her small, stacked heel, Alix headed toward the elevator. The car, when it arrived a minute later, was almost packed.

"We'll wait for another car," she said, when one of the women in the front began to step back.

Before she could retreat, Alix felt her elbow being cupped. Terrance was gently ushering her into the car.

"It's too crowded," she protested.

"We can manage." He flashed a smile at Alix, then proceeded to make a space for the two of them. "Everyone hold your breath," he instructed cheerfully.

She felt his body press against hers as the doors shut. She was acutely aware of every inch of him. Acutely aware that she was reacting to the feel of him despite all her best efforts not to.

What made it worse was she could feel his every

breath as he drew it in and then exhaled. It created shock waves along her skin.

The short ride to the basement felt endless.

Damn him, she thought, frustrated. After all this time, he still had that effect on her of making her feel as if every part of her was coming unglued.

Why was he doing this to her? Why had he come back after all this time, popping up in her life as if he'd only been gone for a weekend instead of six years?

She felt him shift behind her. He'd done this on purpose, she thought. Why, she wasn't sure—maybe to show her that he could still arouse her, that he could still make her want him. No amount of denying it on her part could negate it.

She was far from happy about this. And far from happy to discover that he could still make her feel weak in the knees just by his close proximity.

How the hell was she going to be able to maintain a barrier when he could so easily scramble her thoughts and her pulse?

The doors opened. Alix all but dashed out, taking in the air, recycled though it was, as if it were life affirming.

"Alix—" he began.

"Let's keep this professional, shall we?" she said tersely.

"I've heard other doctors call you by your first name," he told her.

She hurried around a group of three nurses who were moving too slowly. "Yes, but they're my friends."

"I was your friend once," he reminded her.

"The key word here is *once*," she said. "Let's get this over with." Picking up her pace, Alix strode through the corridor toward the cafeteria and its protective hum of noise.

Terrance made no effort to fall in place beside her. Instead he allowed her to get ahead of him, because it gave him a couple of moments to try to figure out what the hell he was going to ask her once they were seated.

Whatever it took just to be semialone with her.

Chapter 5

Because of the hour, the food service area of the cafeteria was fairly empty. Just beyond, in the dining area, only half the tables were occupied. It wasn't nearly as full as she had hoped.

Still, Alix told herself, it was better than hurrying across the street to the outdoor café with Terrance and sitting at one of those tiny tables, so close that their knees touched and their breaths mingled.

It was bad enough being in the same room.

Terrance handed her a tray and then took one for himself, instinctively knowing that Alix would balk at the idea of their sharing one tray.

He'd gotten good at nuances, he thought. One of the by-products of his job. But then, there'd been a time when he'd known everything about her, every thought in her head before it was even completely formed.

He found himself missing that.

There was a small selection of desserts still left on the glass display shelves beside the coffee urn. Terrance nodded at them. "Want anything besides coffee?"

She watched black liquid pour into her cup as she held down the spigot. "To get back to the E.R."

Terrance grinned, picking up a cup and filling it to the brim. "Dr. Beauchamp was right. You are a workaholic."

She looked at him sharply. "You discussed me with Dr. Beauchamp?"

Her tone of voice warned him. "It was the other way around. There's a difference," he pointed out. "We sat here in the cafeteria earlier. He extolled your virtues to me." He looked at her, remembering. "Not that he had to. It was rather like preaching to the choir."

Alix said nothing as she placed her filled cup on her tray and turned around toward the cashier's desk. There was nothing she could say. He was uttering empty words, words she would have cherished once had she not known what she did now. That his words meant nothing. And that she couldn't allow herself to let hope cloud her vision.

Terrance was right behind her in line, his tray

butted up against hers as they pushed both along the metal rungs to the cashier.

"Two," he told the woman on the stool, indicating both trays.

Alix dug into the pockets of her lab coat, looking for money. "I'll pay for my own, thank you."

Terrance already had his wallet out. "A cup of coffee isn't going to break me." He knew what she was thinking. "And it's hardly a bribe." He handed the cashier a five then waved away the change. "When did you get this uptight?"

"The minute you walked up to the podium last week." Not allowing him any time to respond, Alix picked up her tray and walked into the dining area.

He felt it prudent to let her scout out the table, allowing her to feel in control.

Rather than a booth, she chose a free-standing table located in the middle of the cafeteria. It was right in the way of foot traffic, both coming and going. There wasn't a private thing about it.

She thought it was perfect.

Putting her tray on the table, Alix sat down. Then, like a soldier bracing herself for enemy fire, she squared her shoulders and looked at him.

"All right, so what are all these questions about the hospital you have to ask me?"

He'd gone undercover countless times, told lies with the ease of a silver-tongued con artist, sometimes with death only inches away. Why was he having trouble coming up with a simple question for her?

As he set down his tray, his mind was still scrambling for something plausible to ask her that wouldn't cause Alix to get up and walk out. He picked his way through the words carefully, watching her face for warning signs.

"Actually, it's more about the hospital and my career."

She held the cup between both hands and looked down into it. The overhead light made the surface shimmer hypnotically—like the sound of his voice had once done to her. But no longer. "Ah yes, your career. How is your career?"

He smiled to himself, taking a sip of the dark brew. "You know, if you were any more sarcastic, I could probably see little applauding devils surrounding you."

She glanced up at Terrance. "Now who's being sarcastic?" And why, when he smiled like that, did her stomach still quiver a little? You'd think, once you had the disease and gotten over it, you'd be immune to catching it again.

"I prefer to call it observant." He decided to follow a logical progression of events. If he were a newly transplanted doctor, he'd want to be on his own and the sooner the better. "I'm looking to set up a practice. Know anyone who would be interested in taking on a junior partner?"

He meant her, she realized. After all, they were both pediatricians. A wave of heat passed over her. Once, the thought that they both gravitated toward the same area of medicine had filled her with a feeling of contentment. Now there was only a sense of panic threatening to rise up.

Her grip tightened around her cup. "Not off-hand." Her tone was disinterested. "But I'll ask around. Anything else?"

She looked ready to leave. He knew that he should let her. That his feelings for her had nothing to do with this investigation, would only get in the way of that investigation.

But for the moment there was nothing happening on that front, and although he'd seen William Harris at a distance—lecturing a nurse who hadn't brought him a chart quickly enough—he hadn't been able to get close to the man without appearing to force the matter. That kind of thing took a little time. So, just for the moment, he allowed himself to indulge this overwhelming need he was suddenly feeling, a need to attempt to mend at least part of the fences he'd knocked down when he'd left her so abruptly.

He leaned forward, his eyes fixed on hers. "Talk to me, Alix."

Her lips thinned. "I was under the impression that's what I was doing."

She always could parry and thrust, he thought. "I mean talk *to* me, not *at* me." He was losing her.

And he didn't want to. Not before he made amends. Terrance tried again. "Would it help to say I was sorry?"

This was getting them nowhere, she thought in exasperation. And she had patients to see. "Nothing you have to say would help," she told him frankly. "Look, what was, was. Nothing can change that. We're two entirely different people now."

It was both the truth and a lie at the same time. Their paths had split and diverged six years ago, taking them to different places. She'd become a wife, a widow and a mother, all without Terrance. And yet, he'd never left the center of her heart, no matter how hard she tried to bury him.

She'd always felt guilty about that, guilty about not being able to render her whole heart to Jeff, who had deserved better. Her only saving grace was that Jeff knew nothing about the way she'd once felt about Terrance. She never mentioned him to Jeff. He'd died never knowing that her whole heart didn't belong to him. But the sad fact of life was, though she tried very hard, after Terrance had left, she was incapable of surrendering herself completely.

She'd given Jeff as much of herself as she could. But not all.

Maybe she had the wrong idea, Terrance thought. He resisted the desire to take her hand, but it wasn't easy. "I'm not here to pick up where I left off."

"Good," Alix cut in tersely, "because you can't."

"But I don't want there to be this animosity between us."

Alix could feel her jaw tightening. "There's *nothing* between us. No emotion, *nothing*." She was lying and he knew it, she thought. "All right," she finally admitted, struggling to keep her voice down. "Maybe I am a little resentful. Damn it, you walked out on me. Walked out without so much as a word," she accused, "not even goodbye."

He wanted to touch her, to hold her. But he couldn't, not here. Most likely not ever. "I couldn't say goodbye."

Words, they were just words. All after the fact. "But you could leave."

Suddenly he wanted to make her understand, really understand. "I *had* to leave."

"Why? Why did you have to leave?" It didn't make sense then, it didn't make any now.

He blew out a breath, surprised by all the pent-up emotion he felt within him. He'd thought everything had been tidily swept away. Maybe he didn't know himself at all. "Because medicine didn't make sense anymore. Nothing made sense anymore."

She forgot promises she'd made to herself not to be drawn in. Words long held back stormed the gates. "Look, I know how much your father's death affected you, but you could have come to talk to me.''

It hadn't been that simple. He hadn't wanted to bring her down as well. "I couldn't talk to anyone.''

She felt as if he'd just slapped her. "I wasn't just 'anyone.' I was the woman you'd promised to spend the rest of your life with.'' She was fighting back tears, she realized, and prayed she could win the battle. "I was the woman who loved you more than anyone or anything else in this world.''

Compassion and shame filled him, obstructing everything else. He reached for her hand. "Alix—''

She jerked it back as if his fingers were hot branding irons. Damn it, she'd said too much. With a huge effort, she quickly backtracked, trying to restore the blurred line she'd drawn in the sand, the one he wasn't supposed to cross over.

"Past tense, Doctor,'' she said icily. "I'm using past tense.''

Suddenly there were questions, so many questions, and they all centered on her. "Tell me about past tense, Alix,'' he coaxed. "What happened after I left?''

I went to pieces. When I couldn't find you, I thought I'd literally go crazy. Or die. I did neither. I continued. In a world without you, I continued.

Taking a breath, she looked past his head and fixed her attention on a corner of a vending machine. It was easier to talk that way.

"I went on with my life. With the plans I made."
She'd caught herself in time not to say "the plans
that we made."

"My father was extremely helpful," she continued. It was because of her father that she had gone
into medicine in the first place. He was a family
physician, beginning back in the days when they
still referred to the position as being a general prac-
titioner. He'd gotten her involved in medicine from
a very early age. It was all she could remember ever
wanting to be—besides Terrance's wife. "He took
me in as a partner, then helped me get started on
my own." She shrugged, winding up her narrative.
"I met Jeff, we got married and had a little girl."

His eyes never left hers. "Why did you name her
Julie?" If she lied, he would know.

"I always liked the name." She found she
couldn't look away. "And I always liked your
mother." And she had, too. They had gotten along
so beautifully, and for a while she'd had great hopes
that in marrying Terrance, she would have finally
gained a mother, as well. "Her death hit me hard,
too."

He knew that. Just as it had hit him and his father.
Terrance always suspected that was why Jake
McCall had lost his edge. Why that sniper's bullet
had managed to find him while he'd been on the
stakeout. Because his father had already lost his
heart three months earlier when the light of his life

had gone out and his wife had died, a victim of a drunk driver.

Something stirred within Alix despite all her best efforts. The look in his eyes, just for a split second, looked so terribly sad. She almost reached out to touch his face in silent compassion. But grief was no excuse for having done what he'd done.

There *was* no excuse.

She'd been frantic and beside herself those first few months, positive that something sinister had befallen him, because he'd dropped off the face of the earth without so much as a trace. Even when the police had told her that Terrance had packed his clothes and taken his car—all of which pointed to a man making a rational decision—she'd been completely convinced that he was the victim of foul play.

What a fool she'd been. *How many times do I have to be a fool because of you, Terrance?*

Rousing herself, she focused on what he was saying.

"I'm sorry about Jeff," Terrance mustered a note of sincerity he only partially felt. "I didn't know him, but I'm sure he was a very good man. You shouldn't have had that much grief in your life."

"No," she agreed, banking down another wave of emotion, "I shouldn't have. But I went on." She remembered something she'd heard from a popular movie. "Like the man said, you either get busy with the business of dying, or you get busy with the business of living. I had a daughter, a father and a practice. My choice was made for me.'' She was breaking her own rules, telling him this. Determined to turn the tables, she looked at Terrance. ''What about you? Where did you go after your father's funeral?''

He thought for a moment. ''I'm not even sure at first.''

The month that followed his rude awakening that medicine was not the answer to everything, he'd just driven endlessly, staying at motels along the way, trying to find answers in his head. Bypassing anything that had to do with his heart because that route was far too painful to revisit.

Eventually his journey had taken him to Washington, D.C., to the very agency his father had dedicated his life to.

It was there that his path suddenly became clear. If he and medicine hadn't been able to save his father, at least he could take his father's place in the scheme of things. He'd become a DEA agent, picking up his father's sword where it had been dropped and wielding it against the many-headed hydra monster that illegal drug importation had become.

Terrance's eyes shifted to Alix's face. He couldn't tell her all that. Couldn't tell her what he was without jeopardizing his operation.

So he told her the lies that some computer wizard at the home office had neatly input into Boston General's data base, the same records and lies that had gone to Dr. Beauchamp when he had applied for a position with Blair Memorial.

"Eventually I wound up in Boston with Thomas." His older brother was a partner in a large law firm there, and though he had stopped to see Thomas on his way to Washington, he hadn't stayed. "Thomas talked me into giving medicine another chance, saying it would be a shame to throw all that effort and education away. He reminded me that for every patient that was lost, there were more that were saved."

A shiver went down her spine as she recognized the mantra they used to say to each other whenever the rigors of the day got to them and their spirits flagged.

Had he come to her, she would have told him that—and so much more. But he hadn't come to her. He had gone from her.

"Several of the doctors at Boston General were Thomas's clients, so he got me an interview with them." Terrance wrapped it up. He absolutely hated having to lie to her. "I joined their staff and stayed there until I came back here."

Which led them back full circle to her nagging question. "Why?"

"Nostalgia." That was what he was feeling, sitting here opposite her. That and a whole lot more that he couldn't even put a name to. "Maybe to make amends if I could."

She wasn't about to go down that slippery slope again, not even with the best set of skis the world had to offer. "Stick with nostalgia."

He caught her wrist, forcing her to look at him. "Alix, I can't make it up to you—"

"No, you can't." She surprised herself at how firm her voice could sound, even while her insides were turning to jelly.

"But I'd like to try." Was she wavering just the slightest bit? Or was that just his imagination?

Her eyes frosted over. "There's no point."

"There's every point," he insisted, refusing to back away. "I didn't know you were an attending at Blair, but I was hoping to try to look you up once I got settled in Bedford."

She didn't want to be looked up or made amends to or anything at all. She wanted to be left alone. It was the only way she could go on coping. "We've moved on. Let's leave it that way."

He'd held her in his arms and made love with her endlessly. Now that he was here, looking at her, he knew he had to give this a try. "Can we at least be friends?"

"I don't think so." *You gave up that right a long time ago.*

He refused to give up so easily. "Would you at least let me try?"

She glanced at her watch. Her untouched coffee

had grown cold. She rose to her feet, picking up her tray. "Our break's over. I'll see you in the E.R., Doctor."

"Right."

Maybe it was better this way, he thought. Starting something now would only end badly. He couldn't let her into his life now any more than he'd been able to let her in before.

With a sigh he rose to his feet. Terrance took his tray to the counter, letting Alix get ahead of him and leave first.

Alix watched the lights of passing cars chase each other across her ceiling. It was the middle of the night and she was wide awake.

Damn him, she thought angrily, damn Terrance for coming back, for messing with her mind and throwing her whole world off-kilter. Again. Once should have been the limit.

No one can hurt you if you don't let them.

That had been her father's advice to her when her heart had been breaking all those years ago. His advice had been harder to take than he could have dreamed. She hadn't wanted to be hurt, certainly hadn't wanted to pine for Terrance when he so obviously hadn't been pining for her, but it had taken almost a superhuman effort for her to shed both feelings from her life.

That first year without him had been hell. Each

year had been a little easier, but it had all taken time and effort.

Blankets tangled up around her legs, she kicked them free as she turned on her side.

Nostalgia, was it?

Well, he damn well knew where he could put his nostalgia. She wasn't about to allow him to undo six carefully crafted years just because he decided to come strolling back into her life.

Taking a deep breath, she smoothed down the covers on either side of her. She would get through this ordeal, she promised herself. And once Terrance had the lay of the land under his belt, he'd be on his own. Beauchamp had made a point of telling her that the assignment was for a month. That meant she had less than three weeks left. She could do it.

And after that, she thought as she punched her pillow, the man could go to hell.

If not before.

Pleased with her pronouncement, she closed her eyes.

"Mommy..."

Alix's eyes flew up.

"Mommy..."

She heard her daughter's voice floating to her from down the hall.

Oh, well, she wasn't really about to get any sleep tonight, anyway. Which meant that she welcomed the diversion her daughter provided.

Throwing off the covers, Alix got up.

Chapter 6

"Anything bothering you tonight, honey?" Daniel DuCane glanced at his daughter just before he opened his refrigerator for another round of beers. The men sitting around the green felt gaming table in his recreation room had asked for seconds the instant Daniel had gotten up.

"No."

Alix ripped open a jumbo bag of potato chips a little too forcefully. Chips went flying in every direction before she managed to shut the bag again, containing the rest. Algernon, her father's twelve-year-old golden retriever, who had been sleeping on the tile floor immediately came to life. He ran across the floor, eager to help himself to the bounty scattered around him before it was cleared away.

Alix sighed as she looked down at the mess. "Why do you ask?"

Daniel nodded his head at the fallout. "That, for one."

Setting the bottles of beer down on the gray granite kitchen counter, he crossed to where she was standing. Compacting his large frame, he crouched down beside her and began picking up the chips that Algernon hadn't managed to suck in yet.

"You seem preoccupied. Where's that famous Alix banter? I'd think after a week's hiatus," he said, referring to the fact that she'd passed on their weekly game last week, "you'd be back in royal form, flattering the egos of a roomful of old men who dote on you." Daniel chuckled, slanting a look at his daughter as he rose to his feet again. "Half of whom can remember diapering you."

"Thanks, Dad," she cracked. "I needed that image."

Usually being around her father's cronies did have a knack of making her feel young and carefree, temporarily removing the weight she normally carried on her shoulders. In her opinion, playing in the weekly poker game that had gone on since she was a little girl was better than spending a weekend at a spa, being massaged and pampered.

But right now, not even fending off Tyler Mack's flirtation made her forget what was going on in her daily life.

She was surprised her father hadn't already heard. Granted he was rarely at Blair these days, but still, he had friends there and got together with them on a regular basis. She would have thought that someone would have told him about "the new pediatrician."

Alix tossed the chips she'd picked up into the garbage beneath the sink and then dusted off her hands. She turned around to look at her father. "You're not much on hospital gossip, are you?"

She got his attention. He'd always been subtly protective of her.

But before he could say anything, he heard someone enter the kitchen. "Someone gossiping about you, Alley-girl?"

She looked over her shoulder toward the doorway and saw Roy Zane, Bedford's first retired homicide detective, walking in. Sixty-eight, with snow-white hair and a gut that threatened to snap his struggling size forty belt, there was still a twinkle in his eye when he woke up each morning.

Roy put a fatherly arm around her shoulders. "Just tell me who. I'll have Roy Jr. bring him in and scare the pants off him."

Daniel shook his head, taking out another bag of chips from the pantry. He and Roy had been best friends since before either had met their future wives, had been each other's best man and stood by each other when each had buried his wife. They were closer than brothers.

"More taxpayer money put to good use," Daniel quipped, tossing the bag to Alix. "Try not to distribute those quite so liberally."

"Hey, Bedford's got a homicide detective with no homicides to investigative for the most part," Roy protested. It was no secret that he was proud enough to burst that his son had followed in his footsteps and joined the force. "Gotta keep himself busy somehow."

Daniel raised his deep-blue eyes, indicating the doorway. "This was a private conversation, Roy." Picking up the bottles he'd set down, Daniel handed them to Roy. "Go water the players," he instructed.

Roy clutched all five bottles against his chest. "Don't have to tell me twice." But as he began to leave, he paused to look at Alix. "Remember, you need anything, you know who to ask."

She smiled, touched at the older man's concern. "Yes, I do."

Daniel waited until Roy was well clear of the kitchen. He looked at his only child seriously. "*Do* you need anything, Alix?"

"Maybe a breather."

She looked up at her father. Still a handsome man at sixty-five, with a full head of hair and a waistline that had thickened only slightly over the years, he would have been well within his rights to retire like most of the men in the other room. But he still kept his hand in, reducing his patient load and coming in three times a week. He shared his office with a much younger man who was filled with the same enthusiasm Daniel had had when he'd graduated medical school. Warren Kline took up the slack, but her father was always available for consultation. She figured they'd probably bury her dad with his lab coat on and his stethoscope in his hand.

"You were saying about gossip?" he prodded.

She debated not telling him at the last moment, then decided against it. There were no secrets between them. Now would be a poor time to start. "Terrance McCall is back."

Daniel's face sobered considerably. He could remember the agony Alix had gone through when Terrance had just disappeared without warning. Never one to complain, she'd surprised him by breaking down in front of him. He'd never felt so helpless, so impotent in his life. Terrance had broken his daughter's heart and he'd wanted to cut the former's out as payback. Vengeful stuff for a man who went out of his way not to step on a spider.

"And?" Daniel coaxed gently, swallowing the offer to bring her Terrance's head on a platter.

And I don't know if I'm coming or going, Dad. I want to hate him, to block out everything I ever felt about him, but I can't.

Alix tried to summon a smile. "And Dr. Beauchamp asked me to show him around the hospital, to act as his 'mentor' until he gets his 'hospital legs.'" Her lips barely curved at her own quip.

Daniel searched her face. He knew it better than his own, knew what every nuance on it meant. But she was shutting him out. "What does he have to say for himself?"

She shrugged, looking away. "That he's sorry."

Her father laughed shortly. "I'm sure he is. The man walked out on the best thing in his life, the day he left you."

This time she did smile. Thank God for her father. What would she have done without him all these years? He never judged, always supported. What other father would have taken her to a mother-daughter gathering in junior high school? The man was one of a kind.

"Not that you're prejudiced or anything."

"Totally impartial," he agreed. And then he tried to second-guess her thoughts. "Alix, you want me to talk to Clarence for you? Have him hand off the baby-sitting assignment to someone else?"

That would be running, and she didn't run. Not ever. "No."

He smiled. "I didn't think so. Stubborn, like your mother." He sighed. After all these years, he still missed her. "Couldn't get her to listen to reason, either. Is he here for good?"

Again she shrugged. Picking up the kitchen scissors, she cut the bag of potato chips rather than rip it. Algernon gave up waiting for a free handout and trotted back to his corner to sleep.

"He says so."

Daniel took his cue from her tone. "But you don't think so."

She sighed, pouring the chips into the bowl she'd brought in. "I don't know what to think, not when it comes to Terrance."

"One day at a time, honey, that's all we can do. Just one day at a time." He paused as he picked up the refreshed bowl of chips. Algernon raised his head in a last-ditch attempt for more handouts. The animal looked up at him with mournful brown eyes that seemed to say he hadn't eaten in two weeks. "You already had yours," he told the dog.

Algernon lowered his head and laid it on his paws. The animal seemed to sigh.

"Alg," Daniel called to the pet. The dog was instantly alert. "Catch." He threw two chips into the air, neither of which ever completed their arc. Instead, they disappeared behind doggy lips as the animal leaped up to catch his own version of fast food. Daniel laughed, then turned his attention back to Alix. "I can talk to Terrance for you if you'd like. Ask him questions you can't."

"There's nothing I can't ask him, Dad. But he left me," she pointed out. "The answers don't matter."

He looked at her pointedly. "Maybe they should matter." When she looked at him in surprise, he added, "Just a friendly suggestion."

Maybe he was right, Alix thought, taking a couple of beers out for herself and her father. But she didn't want to think about that just now.

"Okay everyone," she announced, coming back into the room. "I've been letting you slide. Now let's get down to some serious poker playing."

The hooting comments that met her challenge warmed her heart.

"I heard we had new blood. Thought I'd introduce myself before the grind got to you."

Terrance was completely aware that the slightly shorter man standing before him in the first-floor hospital corridor was taking measure of him from head to foot. Whenever possible, William Harris covered his more than slight inferiority complex with a rampaging display of superiority.

He extended his hand to him, king to vassal. "Dr. William Harris."

Terrance took the hand that was offered, shaking it firmly. "Yes, I know. Terrance McCall."

A quizzical brow rose on the handsome face. "Someone point me out?"

Terrance wondered how much it took to feed the man's ego and if it was insatiable the way he'd heard. "Dr. DuCane." He slipped his hands back into his pockets. "She's overseeing my initialization here."

At the mention of Alix's name, an expression that could only be termed a subdued leer slipped over Harris's lips. It rankled Terrance instantly.

"Ah, yes, Alix." Harris nodded. "The unscalable citadel."

Terrance kept his annoyance out of his voice, but it wasn't easy. "What do you mean by that?"

There was mild disdain in Harris's voice, as well as disbelief. "She's one of the few women in the hospital who's turned me down."

That just shows she has taste, Terrance thought, maintaining his impassive expression. "Maybe she's not ready to date yet. I heard that she was just recently widowed."

"Not all that recently," Harris contradicted. "Besides," he hooted, "this isn't turn-of-the-century India where the wife gets thrown on her dead husband's funeral pyre. She doesn't seem to know how to have a good time."

Terrance bit back the desire to tell Harris that she wouldn't be seen with scum like him. It wasn't any business of his who she went out with, even someone like Harris. He reminded himself that he was trying to strike up a friendship with Harris, not have the man drawn and quartered.

Nonetheless, it was a tempting thought.

"Then why bother asking her out?"

Harris looked at him incredulously. "Man, have you *seen* that body of hers?"

Terrance realized he was clenching his fists within his lab coat. Beauchamp had been too kind when he'd alluded to Harris's shortcomings. There was something overwhelmingly offensive about the grandson of the founder of the hospital. He was going to thoroughly enjoy bringing him down.

"No," Terrance lied, "I haven't. She wears a lab coat most of the time."

The leer came into full bloom. "I saw her at a fund-raiser for the hospital last year. She was wearing this clingy, off-the-shoulder number that made your mouth water and your knees weak." He shrugged carelessly, as if to show he was relatively unaffected. "Personally, I think the woman gets off being a tease."

Making his prime suspect eat his own teeth before a bust went down was definitely not in his job description, but Terrance was beginning to give serious thought to penciling it in. He knew enough computer hackers to make the line a reality if he really set his mind to it.

But jeopardizing the operation was definitely *not* part of his agenda, so he swallowed the flippant retort that begged to come out. Terrance deliberately changed the subject before he separated Harris's head from the rest of him. "What do Blair physicians do for fun around here after hours?"

Harris rubbed his hands together. "Get together with Blair nurses." He flashed an engaging grin.

Terrance could see how some women might find the other man attractive. He was tall, with dirty-blond hair and an almost pretty face. None of which had helped with his heavy debts to casino bosses.

"But if you're really asking, there's a club just a mile up the road. Gallagher's. That's where the in crowd goes to knock off steam." Terrance assumed that the "in crowd" meant anyone who chose to emulate Harris. "Tell you what," Harris was saying, "I'm off at four. What are you doing tonight?"

Getting close to my primary suspect. A reliable informant had given Harris's name as the unwitting front man in the drug trafficking that was going on. The fact that the informant had turned up dead three days later only served to underscore the reliability of his information.

"Nothing I know of," Terrance answered.

"Great. I'll meet you at the lockers—"

Harris's attention was momentarily diverted by a particularly supple-looking woman who hurried down the corridor to the hospital's gift shop. Harris gave Terrance the impression that he would have followed the woman had he been alone.

Harris glanced at him pointedly. "Unless something comes up, of course."

"Understood."

Just as Harris was about to say something else,

his pager went off. Harris looked at it, annoyed at the intrusion. "Damn it, they think they own you. Looks like I'd better play the dutiful doctor." He laughed dryly. "See you at four."

It was only as Harris went off in search of the nearest phone that Terrance became aware that he was being watched. Alix was at the other end of the corridor. He could see her disapproving look all the way from across the floor.

Was that aimed at him or Harris? Or both?

Terrance lost no time in closing the distance between them. He was beside her before she had a chance to walk away. "Something wrong?"

She'd been there long enough to observe what appeared to be budding camaraderie between two men who in her opinion couldn't have been more different. "Just thinking about how little I really know you."

Had she somehow stumbled onto what he was actually doing here? He doubted it because the agency had been thorough, but Alix was a woman of many talents and gifts. He felt like a man tiptoeing across a tightrope strung over the Grand Canyon.

"And this would be in reference to...?"

She'd already wasted too much time watching him. Alix began walking back to the E.R.

And to think she was beginning to believe that

her father might have had a point. "I didn't think you were the type, that's all."

He didn't particularly like talking to a moving target. Reaching out, he put his hand on Alix's shoulder to stop her. "The type to what?"

She glared at him. Why was he sucking up to Harris? Was he trying to get in with the man's father in order to further his career? Who *was* this man she had once loved so fiercely? "The type to try to cull favor with William Harris."

Terrance didn't like the look on her face when she said that. It made him feel as if he should be heading for the showers. "And what makes you think I was trying to cull favor?"

She'd thought that rather obvious. "William left looking smug, a little like the devil when he's gotten a new soul."

This was ridiculous, arguing over a man obviously neither one of them could abide. He decided to probe a little. "You don't sound as if you like him."

"I don't care for his manner," she replied carefully. She was no longer sure she could trust Terrance with anything.

He shook his head. "The feeling's not returned, you know. He sounded as if he had designs on you."

She searched his face, trying to see if that fact

bothered him the least little bit. But she couldn't see any indication that it did.

How many ways are you going to set yourself up for a fall, Alix?

She shrugged away the comment. "That's only because he can't believe that any woman wouldn't find him irresistible."

"But you don't." He realized he was pushing the envelope, but he wanted to hear her tell him that neither Harris's looks nor his position in the hospital hierarchy held any attraction for her.

She laughed quietly. "Not if he were the last man on earth."

Terrance couldn't help smiling at the declaration. "Well, that's a relief."

She stopped walking again to look at him. "Why?"

The smile turned into a grin. "I thought that honor belonged to me."

"For you the boundaries are stretched." She could see that he wasn't following her. "Not even if you were the last man in the universe."

"Ouch." Terrance pretended to wince. "So much for my ego."

"You never used to have one." That was one of the things she had liked about him.

"I still don't." He winked. "It was just a figure of speech."

She nodded, her mouth curving involuntarily. "I see."

He recalled how much he loved seeing her smile slip into her eyes. "So do I."

Pausing, Alix cocked her head, not following him. "What?"

"You're smiling," he told her. "And hell hasn't frozen over, and I haven't been drawn and quartered."

She laughed. For a single moment it was like old times. "The day is still young."

He looked at her for a long moment. Remembering. "Alix—"

She couldn't quite read his tone. "Yes?"

He lowered his voice as an orderly passed by, pushing a patient on a hospital gurney. He knew she wouldn't appreciate anyone else overhearing what he had to say. "I've missed you."

Alix sobered a little. "I wasn't the one who left."

"No, you weren't." He should have handled it differently, but there was no redoing the past. "What'll it take for you to forgive me, Alix?"

Somehow, *never* had taken on far too large proportions. She shrugged, "Give me time. I'll come up with something."

"Anything," he said to her seriously, then allowed a slight smile to curve his mouth. "Except jumping into a vat full of snakes."

"Still afraid of snakes?"

"I prefer to think of it as maintaining a healthy respect for their territory."

He could still make her laugh, she realized. "I'll keep that in mind." She saw the new orderly, Riley Sanchez, pushing one of the portable X-ray machines out of the E.R. area. It brought her back to reality. "Right now, Doctor, I believe that there are patients in the E.R. in need of your gentle, healing touch."

He smiled to himself, thinking that maybe he'd reached a turning point with her. At least he didn't feel as if he had to dig himself out of ten feet of ice.

He ignored the knowing look that Riley flashed at him just before the latter turned the corner.

Chapter 7

Gallagher's was a warm, friendly bar, the kind that would have been called a pub had it been located across the ocean. Open to everyone, a large part of the clientele who frequented the establishment each evening came from Blair Memorial. Staff went there to talk over a warm beer and nuts that were overly salted, or to just wind down.

For the most part everyone got along, and it was like being part of a club. But every club had its unpopular members and Gallagher's had Harris.

It didn't take someone who attended MENSA to figure out why Harris was disliked. Several minutes into the evening, Terrance could pick up on the vibrations Harris both gave off and attracted. He was inclined to share the general consensus of the swelled-headed physician.

Dr. William Edward Harris was, in Terrance's opinion, a poor excuse for a human being, one of those people who roamed the earth and caused others to scratch their heads and wonder what God had been thinking at the moment of the man's creation.

Terrance shook his head as the bartender approached him, scotch bottle in hand, ready to refill his drink. He was still nursing the one he had.

Coming with Harris to Gallagher's had been the first step in laying the initial foundation for the tentative friendship that was necessary in order to get close to the man. Harris seemed almost pathetically eager to show off for him.

Harris's dossier, which resided within Terrance's laptop at the hotel, said that the doctor had no real friends, just various people who for one reason or another tolerated his presence because of his family. Harris was intelligent enough to know this and to use it to his advantage whenever possible. That meant securing favors, easy women, recreational drugs and, in general, getting people to look the other way whenever he transgressed. Which was often.

But in the past year, it had gone beyond that. Harris, according to their late informant, had gone from the minor leagues of the spoiled to the big leagues. He played hardball with the upper echelon of drug lords, both within the U.S. and outside of it, most notably Colombia.

Not that Harris moved within those circles as a player, but rather as a dupe, a scapegoat who was used just as he used others. The trap designed by the bosses at the casino he favored had been snapped around Harris quickly and efficiently. All because of the man's inability to know when to quit and to push himself away from the gaming tables.

Raising his glass to his lips, Terrance studied Harris. He was sitting on the bar stool beside him as he appeared to drink in his every word. It wasn't easy hiding his contempt for someone who dirtied his own house the way Harris was doing, but that was what they were paying Terrance for.

In over his head, Harris was not only putting his own mediocre reputation on the line, but jeopardizing the hospital's, as well, not to mention running the risk of dragging down his family with him. Obviously, he was oblivious to all of it.

Terrance had no use for people like that.

He looked down at his glass, wishing he had three shots in him rather than less than half of one. He'd been sitting here for the better part of four hours, listening to Harris call out to various people as they entered, all of whom returned his greeting with little enthusiasm.

Terrance was reminded of the line he'd read somewhere about suffering fools in silence—and in his own case, with patience. He had a feeling that someone had suffered a great deal because of this fool beside him.

He nodded at something Harris said to him, pretending to agree, his mind busily creating plans that had nothing to do with what his quarry was talking about. He needed to get Harris to trust him, to think of him as someone he could confide in. Blessed with the kind of face and manner people spilled their secrets to, Terrance felt it was his job to uncover just how deeply entangled Harris was in this drug operation and exactly what part the hospital played in everything. He also needed to know who else at Blair, if anyone, was involved.

His superiors had asked him to "try to keep the hospital's name out of it." Blair Memorial held a venerated spot in the heart of the community.

So now he was not only a DEA agent, but a magician, as well, Terrance mused. And a man who had quite unexpectedly come face-to-face with his past.

Not one of his best assignments, Terrance had to admit, taking another sip of his drink.

Leaning over the bar as if to get a better look at his face, Harris frowned at him disdainfully. "No offense, McCall, but you drink like a wuss."

Terrance smiled amiably. "I have to drive home. I hear the Bedford police frown on people driving on the wrong side of the road around here."

Harris snorted as he signaled for the bartender to fill his glass. "Don't worry, I've got pull. I can have your license restored just like that." After one failed attempt, he managed to snap his fingers. The sound was lost in the noise around them.

Terrance gave a philosophical shrug of his shoulder. Out of the corner of his eye, he saw Riley working a section of the bar. He wondered if the amount of information his partner was gathering exceeded the number of phone numbers he collected. Knowing Riley, it was probably dead even.

"Better not to lose it in the first place."

"A homily." Harris threw back his whiskey, closing his eyes as if savoring the hot burn as it went down. His speech was beginning to sound a little slurred. "How drolly provincial of you, McCall."

"One of us should stay sober," Terrance pointed out. Harris had been drinking steadily since they'd sat down at the bar.

Harris leered broadly, eminently satisfied with himself. "If you're volunteering to drive me home, don't bother. I've already got a chauffeur for to-night." Swaying a little, he wrapped his arm around the redhead sitting on the stool beside him. "Veronica's taking me to her place." He turned to plant a solid kiss on her mouth. "Aren't you Veronica?"

The woman laughed, as if she'd just heard something amusing.

They'd be lucky to make it out of the parking lot without killing someone, Terrance estimated. And he couldn't allow Harris to throw his life away— they might not be able to get to the bottom of what promised to be a huge scandal if anything happened to the man. Months of work in the field would be lost.

Terrance smiled easily. "Maybe I'd better drive you both."

Veronica bobbed her head forward to get a better look at him. "What about my car? I don't want to let anything happen to it."

Then you'd better leave it here. "You can call a cab in the morning."

The answer Terrance gave her seemed to satisfy the redhead.

Harris shifted, ready to launch into the second half of his evening. He never moved his arm away from Veronica. "Very sporting of you, McCall." He looked around the room. The motion seemed to make him dizzy. He blinked, focusing. "Why don't you grab a willing blonde or brunette and come along? We can make it a foursome." Harris grinned wickedly. "The more the merrier."

Even if he hadn't read his dossier, Terrance had a gut feeling that he had no interest in the type of things that made William Harris merry. Since joining the DEA, he'd scratched the underbelly of life more than once, but he'd never been comfortable about it. Now, with the reemergence of Alix in his life, unintended through it was, old boundaries he'd once entertained seemed to come into place for him.

He didn't even want to go through the motions of pretending to be interested in another woman. Besides, he had a feeling that a man like Harris wouldn't stand for competition. He was the type who wanted to be the cock of the walk.

Terrance glanced at his watch and shook his head. "Maybe next time. I've got a 6:00 a.m. call in the E.R."

Harris waved away the excuse. "Don't worry about it, I've got Dr. Alix under my thumb." Harris leaned into him and came close to sliding off the stool, righting himself at the last moment. "I'll tell her to cut you some slack. She'll have no choice but to listen to me. What do you say?"

The redhead, Terrance noticed, had a friend. A blonde who was giving him a very thorough once-over. "Better not. Beauchamp is still monitoring me."

"The old coot." Harris finished his drink. "He's two breaths away from retirement." The bottom of his glass hit the bar with a resounding whack, underscoring his point. "I'm going to be running that place someday." He turned to his new companion. "Did you know that, Victoria?"

"Veronica," she corrected.

"Yeah, whatever." He continued without missing a beat. "Someday I'll get to roam around that hospital, making speeches and getting a slice of the bigger pie, just like my old man and his old man before him. Noblesse oblige—or something like that," the man mumbled under his breath, completely misinterpreting the term as he lifted up his glass. "Barkeep, hit me," he called.

All things being equal, Terrance had a feeling that there'd be more than one taker for that order.

After one more drink, the bartender cut him off. Harris declared he wouldn't be returning, a threat everyone knew would be forgotten by the end of the next day. As agreed, Terrance drove both Harris and his newfound playmate to her home, a garden complex less than half a mile away from city hall and the police department. Given the circumstances, Terrance found the location rather ironic.

"You know, they really shouldn't make these stairs so steep," Harris complained, holding on to the railing as he made his way up to the second floor and Veronica's apartment. He was buffered by a tipsy Veronica in front of him and Terrance bringing up the rear. "What are you, part mountain goat?"

Veronica giggled again, reaching the landing. She began the hunt for her house keys.

"Here, maybe I can help," Harris mumbled, leaning over. His cell phone came tumbling out of his pocket.

Terrance made a grab for it. "You should be

careful with these things," he warned him, flipping the phone open as if to check it. "They break easy."

"So?" Harris laughed majestically. "I'll get a new one. It's only money."

"So it is," Terrance agreed, handing the phone back to him. It now contained a microscopic electronic device that keep track of all of Harris's calls, both incoming and out. Terrance prided himself on his sleight of hand.

One tap down, one to go, he thought.

The duo disappeared behind Veronica's door without so much as a word.

Terrance lost no time in driving over to Harris's condo. It was located in the most upscale area of a city that possessed no poor section.

That was one of things he remembered liking about Bedford, Terrance thought, as he quickly manipulated the front-door lock. The fact that there were no rundown sections, no so-called "poorer" side of town. All of it, even the less expensive area, was well maintained.

Terrance let himself in.

The man liked the finer things in life, he noted, glancing around. Terrance worked quickly. Finding the master bedroom, he placed a surveillance device on that phone. He made sure that the tap was activated anytime one of the eight phones in the house was picked up.

Harris either spent a hell of a lot of time talking

on the phone, or he had a phobia about missing a call, Terrance mused. He let himself out.

Less than ten minutes had lapsed.

Getting into his car, Terrance looked at his watch. It was after nine, though it felt a great deal later. He knew he should be getting back to the hotel. He needed to write his report and see if there was something he'd missed.

But the car seemed to have a mind of its own. There was no other excuse for why he was suddenly turning down the wrong street, heading in the wrong direction. Allowing his car to drive to Alix's neighborhood.

To Alix's house.

He'd looked up the address earlier, knowing he shouldn't. No earthly good would come of his knowing where she lived, but he needed to. He'd promised himself he wouldn't act on it, he just wanted to know, that was all.

It was the first time he'd lied to himself.

Well, maybe the second, he amended. The first time had been when he'd told himself that eventually he would get over the way he felt about Alix. That hadn't really happened, either.

Alix sighed as indecision waged a minor skirmish in her brain. Standing in the hall just beyond her sleeping daughter's bedroom, she was vacillating

over whether or not she should take a warm, lei-
surely bath or go directly to bed.

A half smile curved her lips.

*Do not pass go, do not collect two hundred dol-
lars, go directly to bed.*

The trouble was she was exhausted and tense at
the same time. Julie had been particularly energetic,
when Alix had come home from the hospital tonight, and although Norma had volunteered to stay
over and take care of her little firecracker, Alix had
sent the housekeeper home. Between her regular
hours and the emergencies that took her away sometimes in the middle of the night, Alix felt as if she
was shirking her responsibilities as a mother. Julie
needed a little one-on-one contact, even if it meant
having it with a woman whose eyes kept closing.

Alix had to admit that she'd regretted her decision
a couple of times during the course of the evening,
especially when Julie gave no indication of tiring
out.

But eventually, mercifully, sleep had to come to
everyone, and her little ball of fire began to extin-
guish slowly until she'd fallen asleep on the sofa
while watching umpteen reruns of *Scooby-Doo.*

It was nice that she and Julie had that in common,
Alix had thought, carrying the precious bundle off
to bed. *Scooby-Doo* had been her cartoon of choice
when she'd been Julie's age. And older.

Nothing like the classics, Alix had mused fondly.

Bath, she suddenly decided. She needed to sink herself into a tubful of hot suds, sweet scent and promises.

The sound of the doorbell stopped her dead in her tracks. Instinct had her glancing at the pager she kept perpetually attached to her waist in case one of her small patients needed her.

Nothing was flashing at her.

No ignored phone number demanded attention. Whoever was on her doorstep hadn't paged her first and there'd been no phone calls this evening, urgent or otherwise, other than a telemarketer trying to talk her into taking advantage of low travel rates.

She debated ignoring the doorbell, but when it rang again, curiosity got the better of her.

"Put away your gun, honey," she called out loudly as she approached the door. "I'll go see who it is."

Standing on tiptoes, she looked through the peephole.

Terrance.

She would have been more prepared to see a pink elephant. Taking a deep breath, she braced herself and opened the door partway.

Terrance looked inside with mild surprise. "You have someone in here with a gun?"

Embarrassed, Alix laughed softly, shaking her head. "I just do that to scare off the wrong kind of people."

He banked down the urge to ask her if she thought of him in that category. "It almost worked. Why don't you get a dog?"

She thought of Algernon. She'd been the one who'd named the animal. "I have a dog—it's at my father's." A small smile flirted with her lips before retreating. "Getting another one would somehow seem disloyal."

A familiar feeling swirled around him. That was so Alix, he thought.

She shifted, not fully prepared to open the door to him. "What are you doing here?"

A pull that could only be described as sexual, no matter how he tried to disguise it, commandeered his body.

Damn but he'd missed her. Missed seeing her like this, soft and feminine, with tousled hair and hints of sleep about her eyes.

He'd missed everything about her.

"Searching for a little sanity," he confessed.

His evening with Harris had left him yearning to touch base with something clean and good. Alix had come to mind instantly. That was why he'd driven here, he realized. To remind himself that the world did not belong to the Harrises and that his job was making it safer for people like Alix.

He looked weary, she thought. Alix stepped back, opening the door wider. *Big mistake,* a small voice taunted. She ignored it.

"Do you want to come in?"

Terrance hesitated, afraid that if he came in, perhaps he wouldn't leave when the time came. He couldn't afford slipups, couldn't afford to be who and what he'd once been, even if he could remember the road back to that elusive place.

"I don't want to keep you from anything."

Again she laughed softly, completely unaware of how the sound affected him, how it made him yearn. "The coach to take me to the ball won't be here for another half hour. I've got time."

Taking a step inside, Terrance looked around. A feeling of well-being seemed to spring up at him instantly. "Nice place."

Alix closed the door quiet behind him, unconsciously chewing on her lower lip. Maybe she should have just told him it was late and shut the door. "I like it."

"It's homey." He turned to look at her. The urge to touch her was very, very strong. He shoved his hands into his pockets. "It suits you."

"So now I'm homey?" What was he doing here, really?

He laughed. Had she taken that as a backhanded compliment? He hadn't meant it that way. "Only in the very best sense of the word."

Suddenly she felt vulnerable. Alix deliberately kept space between them, wondering what had become of her anger. Anger was always a wonderful shield.

Feeling awkward, she gestured toward the kitchen. "Can I offer you something to drink?"

"Soda would be fine." She began to walk off. "Or orange juice. Or water."

She looked at him over her shoulder. "Not hard to please, are you?"

He crossed to her, knowing he should stay put. "Actually, my standards are very high."

Where had all the space between them gone? She was less than three inches from him, remembering what it had felt like to be in his arms. The smile faded from her lips. "Is that why you left?"

"I left because you deserved better."

"I had better." Her eyes searched his face. She had no idea what she was looking for. "I had you. Or so I thought."

He looked at her, thinking that he shouldn't have come. Wishing he could stay.

"Mommy!"

The small voice broke the tension as it floated down to them. Saved by a two-year-old, he thought.

Terrance nodded toward the sound. "You're being summoned. I'd better go."

He was giving her a way out. She knew she should take it. Usher him out and close the door.

Instead, she heard herself asking, "Would you like to see her?"

See her. See a little girl who was the product of a union Alix had had with another man. With a man who wasn't him. "Yes, very much."

"Then c'mon." Turning, she led the way up the stairs and to her daughter's bedroom.

It looked a little like fairyland, he thought when Alix opened the door. He knew instinctively that Alix's bedroom had looked exactly like this when she had been a little girl. With stuffed animals everywhere and storybook characters laughing and playing across light-yellow wallpaper.

And she had probably looked just like the small child sitting up in the junior bed. Long, blond hair cascaded down both shoulders of her pink nightgown as the little girl held out her arms to her mother.

"Bad dream, Mommy," the little girl cried.

She could have been his child, he thought suddenly. If he'd stayed, Julie could have been his. He watched Alix gather the girl to her. Julie curled her body around her like a little monkey. He stood in the doorway, mesmerized. "How old?"

Stroking her daughter's head as she began to rock, Alix looked at him. "Almost two and a half."

"Precious." Terrance ventured in a few steps. "Like her mother."

Alix ignored the comment. What could she say to that? He couldn't mean it. It was just lip service.

Instead she pressed a kiss to the top of Julie's head and asked, "Want me to rock you, monkey?"

"Uh-huh."

Still holding Julie, Alix stood up and crossed to the rocking chair she kept in the corner. She was acutely aware that Terrance was watching her every move.

Sitting down, her arms folded around Julie, Alix began softly singing an old lullaby. The tune was familiar. Terrance recalled hearing it somewhere, although who had sung it wasn't clear.

Something twisted and ached within him as he watched. Again he thought that this could've been his, if he hadn't left.

But it wasn't. And it wouldn't be, he reminded himself. But it did no harm to stand here, pretending. As long as he *remembered* that he was pretending.

Julie cuddled against her and was asleep again in less than five minutes. Alix scooted forward on the seat, watching Julie for any signs of stirring. There were none. Placing a finger to her lips as she looked at Terrance, Alix slowly rose to her feet. With small, almost imperceptible steps, she made her way to the girl's bed again.

Terrance pulled the covers back for her and together they slipped Julie into the bed. For a split second Alix found herself thinking that it seemed they were playing house.

They made their way back to the front door in silence, as if a single word would somehow manage to rouse the child again.

Or maybe it was because neither of them knew what they could say at a time like this.

And then they were at the door.

Sanctuary, Alix thought.

"She's beautiful."

His compliment made her smile with pride, as did everything about her daughter. "Thanks, I think so."

Self-made promises of not touching her to the contrary, Terrance couldn't help reaching out to tuck away a stray stand of her hair behind her ear. "Just like her mother."

Alix pulled her head back. Warning signals shot off salvos through her system.

"Don't start."

Half plea, half order, the whispered words hung between them like a sheer veil, to be torn down or observed.

Terrance struggled to do the latter. "I'm not," he promised.

But even as he was saying it, even as he meant it, Terrance cupped her face with his hand, tilting her head back.

The next heartbeat he brought his mouth down to hers.

Chapter 8

No!

Yes!

Diametrically opposed emotions warred inside
her. Even within the confines of her own mind, Alix
couldn't win the battle that she knew she had to in
order to survive, in order to continue.

But it had been so long, so very long since she
had felt like this. As if there was a fire burning
inside her. A fire that brought her to life. Everything
seemed so much more vivid, so much more real the
instant his lips touched hers. It was as if all this time
she'd been living in a black-and-white world and
now it was in Technicolor.

The years she spent with Jeff dropped away as if

they had been lived by someone else, in another
lifetime. It was Terrance whom she had always
loved with a fierceness that consumed her down to
the very core of her being. Terrance who owned her
whole heart, because she was incapable of loving
with only half.

For a moment Alix gave herself up to the rapture
that had taken hold of her, tears forming within her
eyes. They were tears of joy, of sorrow, of home-
coming.

For this one moment she was his and he was hers.

Terrance felt control slipping away from him. He
couldn't stop himself.

He didn't know what possessed him. Common
sense had always been his mainstay. No matter
what, he'd always been able to think clearly, to act
rationally. That was why he'd left Alix in the first
place, because he'd known that he was undergoing
a transformation, one she would have trouble standing by. She deserved better, and because he loved
her, he'd left so that she could eventually get on
with her life.

But now common sense had somehow burned
away in the heat of these feelings, the way a meteor
burned up entering the atmosphere. There wasn't
even a cinder left for him to reflect on.

Holding her to him, pressing her warm body
against his, Terrance slanted his mouth against
Alix's as memories of what they had once had, of

what they had once been to each other came rushing back to him with a vengeance that shook him down to the bone.

Slowly the small, raised voice penetrated the blazing haze that had wrapped tightly around them.

"Mommy!"

Terrance stopped kissing her at the exact same moment that Alix put her hands against his chest. They both knew this couldn't, *shouldn't* be happening.

Steadying his voice, Terrance looked up toward the stairs. "I guess Julie wasn't as asleep as we thought."

"No," Alix murmured, an ache beginning to grow within her even as she mentally stood back in disappointment at her own weakness. She caught her lower lip between her teeth, unconsciously savoring the taste of him. "I guess she wasn't."

She stood and looked at him for another moment, even though everything within begged her to make good her escape, to seize her reprieve, race up the stairs and offer up a silent prayer of thanks that she had been saved from making a mistake. Because with very little persuasion, she would have surrendered to her feelings and to him and that would have been a huge, huge mistake. For a second, while he'd been kissing her, she'd felt the way she had six years ago.

But it wasn't six years ago, it was now, and she

wasn't the same person she had once been, not anymore. Things had happened, her life had changed.
She had grown and now looked at the world with
eyes that were no longer naive, no longer innocent.

More important, she was a mother now, with responsibilities, not a woman who could just risk everything because her heart told her to.

Not her heart, Alix amended, her body. It was her
body that was reacting to Terrance, succumbing to
the heat that was generated between them. It always
had. They'd become lovers within the first week of
knowing each other. He'd been her first.

You never forget your first.

The phrase echoed in her brain. She couldn't remember when she had heard the sentiment. Was that
all it was, this feeling that had come up and seized
her by the throat, just a trip down memory lane? A
trip to a happier, safer time, when she'd still believed that happily-ever-after was actually an op-
tion?

She didn't know. She didn't know anything. Her
head felt like a piece of Swiss cheese.

"Mommeee."

Terrance nodded toward the stairs. Maybe it was
better this way. For both of them. "You'd better
go."

She nodded, too numb to risk talking again.

"And, Alix?"

She paused, her hand on the doorknob, looking

at him expectantly. Almost afraid of what he might say. Afraid that it might be what she wanted to hear. That he was staying the night.

"Try leaving the light on for her," Terrance advised. "It might help. Being afraid of the dark is an awful thing."

She already knew that. Because she was. It was in the dark that her greatest regrets rose up to seek her out. To taunt her with what wasn't but might have been.

Alix dropped her hand to her side. "Thanks." She took a step away from the door. "You'll let yourself out?"

"I'll let myself out." With that he turned and went out, closing the door behind him.

The sound echoed in her chest.

Alix raced up the stairs to Julie's room, focusing only on her daughter.

"Get anything yet?" Terrance asked the man sitting at the table, wearing state-of-the-art headphones around his neck like some kind of oversize, thick, stretched-out choker.

Slightly overweight, slightly balding, given to bland, nondescript clothing, Monroe Fontaine looked to be ten years older than he actually was. But his mind was cutting-edge sharp, and he had a tolerance for surveillance that was rivaled by none.

Sitting at a desk that was littered with Chinese

takeout cartons, some dating back to the beginning of last week's wiretap operation, Monroe shook his head. "I was going to ask you the same thing."

Terrance looked at the reels of tapes that had begun to gather in the corners, all recording conversations that apparently went nowhere. Just like the investigation. If there was to be a drug drop-off in the immediate future, nobody was talking.

Absently Terrance picked up the tape on top of the pile and read the label. It chronicled time and place. Nobody had a gift for detail like Monroe. Had to drive his wife crazy, Terrance judged. He replaced the tape.

"Only that Harris spends money like water and drinks like a fish."

"That's a fallacy, you know," Monroe contradicted. Endless hours of surveillance provided him with an excellent opportunity to read books no one else would have even thought of spending their time on. "If fish drank the way people imply, they wouldn't have anything to swim around in."

Edgy because of the investigation and because of the added tension he was carrying around with him these days, Terrance said shortly, "That'll come in handy if I'm ever on *Jeopardy.*" Knowing that had to sound sharp, he amended his tone. "So no one's gotten in contact with Harris?"

Monroe was the essence of patience. "If they did,

they weren't calling him on his cell phone or the house number.''

Terrance frowned. It had been hard enough to get a judge to agree to a warrant for a tap on those. They couldn't very well bug every phone in the hospital. He sighed. ''Keep on it.''

''That's what they pay me for.'' Getting up, Monroe moved to the refrigerator. He was still tethered to the voice-sensitive recorder by way of a one-hundred-foot umbilical chord. The contents of the refrigerator didn't seem to brighten his day. He must miss his wife's Italian cooking. ''Hey, Riley stopped by earlier. He tells me you did an emergency tracheotomy the other day. Saved a kid's life. Pretty impressive.''

Terrance thought so. It amazed him just how things came back to him. There'd been no panic when the paramedics came rushing in with the boy, the kid's parents hurrying right behind them. Out of the blue, a clear vision of what he had to do had come to him.

He blessed the fact that he had a photographic memory. Otherwise, it might have been too late by the time Alix reached the exam room. She'd taken over after that, but the save had been his.

Alix.

By and large they were staying clear of each other these days after the incident at her house last week.

He had to admit it was wiser that way. He didn't trust himself around her.

It was a first.

"Lucky it came back to me," he said to Monroe.

The man had no ego problem. Unlike their suspect, Monroe thought. Taking out a can of diet soda, he closed the refrigerator and popped the top.

"So now that you've performed your first miracle, you thinking of becoming a doctor again once this is over?" Tilting the can to his mouth, Monroe studied Terrance over the rim.

This was just an interlude. Catching bad guys was where his heart lay, not medicine. "No, the agency has me for life."

Sitting down again, Monroe shivered. "God, that sounds lonely."

Terrance gave him a playful swat over the head. "Go back to your surveillance. I'll check in with you later."

Taking his leave, Terrance walked through and then out of the unfurnished condo the DEA had rented. Located less than half a mile down the road from Harris's own condo, it allowed Monroe relatively clear visibility of the man's home. He could alert the different teams whenever Harris left the house.

They were covering all the angles, combing the streets for another informant, keeping tabs on Harris. They had men down in Bogota, watching the drug lords and higher ups in the cartel. Something was going to give soon.

It was just a matter of time. And then this would all be behind him.

As would Alix.

There was no doubt in his mind that once the operation went down and his part in it was revealed, she would think he was using her and that he had been lying about everything. In her place he'd probably think the same thing.

It wasn't exactly a good way to jump-start a relationship he now fervently wished he had never allowed to die.

If wishes were horses, then beggars would be kings.

Where had that come from? He had to stop hanging around Monroe, Terrance told himself as he got into his car.

It was all about choices. And he had made his. Now all that remained was to stick by it.

Easier said than done, he thought, starting up his car. It rumbled to life. A hell of a lot easier said than done.

The taps clearly weren't working. They needed something more.

Standing in the doctors' locker room, Terrance looked down at his hand. Nestled in the middle of his palm was something that had once existed only in the realm of fantasy and the better Bond movies. A transmitter so tiny it could fit on the head of pin. Which was exactly where it was. Now all that remained was to plant the same pin on the inside lining of Harris's coat. It might just bring about the change of luck they needed.

Terrance waited until his day was over. He knew that Harris was assisting in surgery. That gave him a little time.

Terrance had made his way to the doctors' lounge and waited for the opportune moment when he was alone. Two of the nurses had hung around what felt like forever until one of them mentioned that Wanda might be looking for them. They took off like two bullets fired from the barrel of the same gun.

The second he was alone, Terrance jumped to his feet and crossed to the lockers. Riley, whom he always believed was a safe-cracker at heart, had gotten him the combination. It saved time.

Opening the door quickly, he found Harris's coat and turned the lining inside out at the base.

He heard the sigh even through the closed door. Slipping, he pricked his finger. Terrance snapped the pin closed and pushed the coat into the closet.

Behind him the door opened. Seeing Terrance standing at Harris's locker, Alix stopped dead.

Her eyes narrowed. Was he going through Harris's things? Why? "What are you doing?"

"Closing Harris's door." Mission completed—

just barely—Terrance shut the locker door quickly. "I noticed it was open."

Alix continued staring at him. Terrance was acting strangely. He had for a while now. The other day she'd come up behind him when he was on the phone. He'd hung up immediately, as if he hadn't wanted her to know who he was talking to. It wasn't the first time.

Was there another woman?

But if there was, what did that have to do with his prowling through Harris's locker?

Terrance crossed to her. She was thinking. He could tell by the way her brow furrowed. "Something wrong? I could hear you sigh right through the closed door."

She lifted her right shoulder in a half shrug, not answering. Instead she went over to the large communal closet and began rummaging. She didn't find what she was after. Exasperation reared its head, threatening to take over. These days it seemed to maintain quarters in close proximity to her. "Have you seen the yellow pages around here?"

He didn't even know the hospital had any in the room. "No, what do you need with the yellow pages?"

She supposed she could always call information. She reached for the telephone on the table. "I need the number of a cab company." She dialed 411, only to have him place his finger on the cradle, cutting her off. "Hey," she protested indignantly.

He knew opportunity when he saw it. "Something wrong with your car?"

She frowned at him. He still had his finger on the cradle. "Yes, my mechanic has it. Norma was supposed to pick me up, but she's running late today and can't come by until later. Later isn't good."

It occurred to him that he should ask why, but all he could think of was that if he took her home, it would give him a chance to be alone with her again. Fate seemed to be conspiring to throw them together and there were times, like now, when he was a great believer in fate.

She pulled the telephone away from him and began to dial again.

Again he cut her off. "I'm off." he told her. "I can take you home."

Sharing a small, enclosed space with him. Not a good idea. "That's all right, I can take a cab."

"You'll have to wait for one," Terrance pointed out. "If you're in a hurry, you'd be better off letting me take you home."

She didn't know about that. "A cab driver won't try to kiss me."

The grin made Terrance look wicked and guileless at the same time. "You never know." And then he became serious. "I'm sorry about the other night, Alix. I was out of line."

"Yes, you were." And then, because it hadn't exactly been a one-way street, she relented. "Neither one of us had any business going there."

Maybe they could still be friends. It was worth a shot. "Look, there's no need to call a cab. I'm perfectly trustworthy." Crossing his heart, Terrance held up his hand in a solemn, silent oath. "If it'll make you feel better, I won't even stop the car. I'll just slow it down. You can leap out onto your lawn. It looked pretty soft."

She laughed at the image that brought to mind. This wasn't exactly some spy movie. "That won't be necessary. You can stop the car."

Terrance smiled as he followed her out. "Then you'll let me take you home?"

Alix ignored the little voice in her head that was yelling Mayday. "I don't have much choice. I am in a hurry."

They took the back corridor, leading to the parking lot restricted to doctors only.

"Hot date?" he teased.

Oh, God, she hoped not. "It's a date. The temperature's not a factor."

She'd decided that going out, getting back into the swing of things again was the best way to fight these feelings she was experiencing for Terrance. Maybe they had come out of loneliness. She hadn't been with anyone since Jeff had died.

Maybe that was all it was, just frustration on her part. At least she could hope.

He pointed out his car and then took her arm, ushering her toward it. All the while, he could feel this tightness in his gut. She was going out with someone.

Well, what did he expect her to do, become a nun? She was young, beautiful and intelligent. He was surprised men weren't laying siege to her house.

"Anyone I know?" He surprised himself at how nonchalant the question sounded.

She slid into the passenger side of the car and stared straight ahead as she answered his question. "William Harris."

About to pull out, Terrance stopped. "I thought you said—"

She knew what she'd said, and if she went over it, she'd allow her second thoughts to take over and call the date off. That wasn't going to happen.

"You seem to find enough redeeming qualities in him to spend almost every evening in his company," she reminded Terrance. The fact that the two men spent time together still surprised her, even though she told herself it shouldn't. After all, what did she really know about this version of Terrance McCall? He seemed so different from the Terrance she'd known six years ago.

And yet...

She forced herself to focus on the conversation. "I thought maybe I'd been too harsh judging him. And he is very persistent." Though, if she hadn't been desperate to shut thoughts of Terrance out, there wouldn't have been any way Harris would have managed to wear her down.

There was a reason for Harris's persistence, Terrance thought. The man just wanted another conquest to soothe his ego. Well, it wasn't going to be Alix. He could protect her and still not compromise the operation.

Terrance slowed down at the next corner as the light turned red. It gave him an opportunity to look at her. "Alix, you're a grown woman—"

"Yes," she agreed, "I am. And as such, I'll do what I want, when I want." Her eyes met his and held. "You taught me all about that."

Now he got it. "If you're going out with him to get back at me—"

She didn't want him to think that any of this was about him—even though it was. That would give him power over her.

"No, I'm going out with him to get back into life. I kissed you the other night because I was lonely, that's all." She looked down at her folded hands. "It took me a long time to get over you, but I'm over you. It's just time I moved on to something else, to someone else."

He noted that she didn't bring her late husband's

name into all this. Was that because the man hadn't counted? Or just that she was so annoyed with him that she'd forgotten about Julie's father?

In any event, he knew that arguing with her would only make her more obstinate and contrary. "Whatever you say, Alix."

She didn't like his tone. "That's right. Whatever I say."

She should have felt triumphant, that she'd won her point. But it bothered her a great deal that Terrance had retreated as quickly as he did. Didn't he care, even the slightest bit? Didn't he care that she was dating another man? That she was dating William Harris?

Of course he didn't. When was she going to grow up and stop having these fantasizes about men? No, not about men, about Terrance.

It was beginning to look like her father was the only faithful, steadfast man God had created. After that, He'd turned his attention to a more inferior mold.

Turning her face forward, she folded her hands in her lap. The rest of the trip to her house was conducted in silence.

Chapter 9

Dusk was beginning to tiptoe in along the streets like a shy bride on her wedding night. The neighborhood children within the development had long since headed back home, to face chores, homework or both.

Terrance shifted in his seat. Next time he was going to have to get a roomier car, he thought, disgruntled. One he could really stretch his legs out in. But then, he hadn't bought the vehicle with long-term confinement in mind.

He glanced down the street. Other than a passing blackbird and the wind tousling the tops of the trees, there was no movement.

He shouldn't be here.

He was, Terrance thought, behaving like some lovesick schoolboy. Trying to placate his conscience by giving himself a load of excuses for his sitting out here was just that: a load of excuses. There was no reason for him to be on the lookout for Harris. If the man was with Alix tonight, then he wouldn't risk making contact with any of the people involved in the drug cartel. Even Harris wouldn't be that stupid.

No, it wasn't the operation that had him out here. What motivated him to be sitting in his car, across the street and down the block from Alix's house was the fact that he didn't trust Harris not to make a move on Alix—a move he couldn't bring himself to believe that she would actually invite.

Which meant that he'd have to somehow find a way to protect her that wouldn't blow his cover.

He blew out a breath, aggravated with her. With himself.

If she wouldn't invite any moves from Harris, then what the hell was she doing going out with the man in the first place? Alix wasn't a casual woman. She didn't just flit from one man to another in search of fun. That wasn't like her.

She didn't—

How the hell did he know what she did or didn't do anymore? he demanded silently. It'd been six years since he'd been with her. Six long years. People changed in six years.

But not Alix.

He couldn't get himself to believe that she would change. Oh sure, she'd gotten more independent, more assertive, but this went way beyond that. It was like saying that a rabbit could become a bat. There was no basis for it in nature.

He argued with himself, getting nowhere and staying put until he saw Harris pull up in Alix's driveway in his flaming-red Ferrari.

"Showtime," he murmured to himself, making sure that the earpiece to the transmitter he had planted in Harris's coat was firmly in place. Thanks to the device, he'd be privy to any conversation Harris and Alix had as long as it was somewhere within range of the coat.

He wasn't sure if that was going to be a blessing or a curse.

Because the device had a range of twelve city blocks, Terrance could keep a safe, undetectable distance behind their car and still not lose them. It came in handy when traffic separated him from the Ferrari for a good ten minutes.

He was hardly surprised when Harris took Alix to the most expensive restaurant in Newport Beach for dinner. The trendy restaurant had been written up in all the latest magazines. Overlooking the beach, it attracted an exclusive clientele. Terrance couldn't help wondering if maybe Harris *was* going

to make some kind of contact with the cartel tonight
and was using Alix for cover.

Anger speared through Terrance even as he told
himself that Harris wasn't clever enough for that.
From all the evidence he'd seen so far, the man was
a shallow dupe, nothing more.

Harris was here, most likely, just to show off.
Undoubtedly trying to dazzle Alix with his money
and his self-inflated ego.

Terrance banked down his temper.

Parking in the lot, Terrance debated going in, then
decided against it. He didn't want Alix to see him
unless it was absolutely necessary. Popping up in
the same place where Alix and Harris were dining
would be just too much of a coincidence not to
arouse suspicion on both their parts.

With a sigh Terrance tried to make himself comfortable as he listened to the conversation within the
restaurant. For the most part, the transmitter filtered
out background noise, but it interfered at times.

He frowned as Harris made a rude remark about
one of the waitresses. Did he think that was going
to impress Alix?

The man was a loser from the word go. What was
Alix doing with him?

It was, Terrance decided, going to be a very long
night.

This had been a mistake, Alix thought, sighing
inwardly as she listened to only half of what Harris

was saying to her. She should never have given in and agreed to see him socially. Her first instincts had been on target. The man had little to no redeeming qualities, despite Terrance's allusions to the contrary. Served her right for being vulnerable, for trying to prove to herself that she was reacting to Terrance only because she'd been so isolated since Jeff's death.

What did Terrance see in Harris? Why did he spend time with him? Everything out of Harris's mouth only turned her off. She'd never met anyone so filled with his own self-importance.

Terrance had spoiled her, she thought ruefully, toying with her dessert. With his unassuming manner and inherent kindness, he'd spoiled her, had made her feel that all men had dignity and manners.

William Harris was living proof that she was wrong.

She pushed back her plate and looked pointedly at the man sitting across from her. Several times he'd tried to put his hand on her knee. When he did it the last time, she'd made up her mind. Time to bring this disaster of an evening to an end.

"William, I think we'd better go."

Harris looked at her, as if trying to decide whether she was being coy or maybe eager. Was she trying to tell him that she wanted him to take her home so that they could get to the meat of the evening?

"What's your hurry? The night's still young. I thought we'd go dancing after this."

The thought of being on a crowded dance floor, giving him an excuse to grind against her was beyond repugnant to her. She would rather lie down covered in honey on an occupied ant colony.

"I don't think that's a very good idea." Alix ran her hand across her brow. "I've got a headache, William. A migraine."

Harris studied her face for a moment. "All right, we can go." He looked around the busy restaurant. "Where the hell is the damn waiter?" Irritation resounded in his voice as he raised his hand in the air and snapped his fingers expectantly.

This had to be penance for something, Alix thought. What had she been thinking, saying yes to Harris? This was definitely *not* the way back to the world of the living. More like burrowing into the world of the damned.

She was embarrassed for him. People were looking. "The food server doesn't materialize when you do that."

He looked at her, a pout on his lips. "At these prices, they damn well better."

To the table's left, Alix saw the server coming their way, a frown momentarily gracing the man's face as he looked at Harris. It disappeared as he approached their table. "Yes?"

"We'd like the check," Harris informed him.

"Separate checks," Alix was quick to clarify. In no way did she want Harris to think that she was beholden to him for anything.

Harris looked horrified. "Absolutely not. This is a date, not an outing."

Alix smiled patiently at him. In her profession she had more than a nodding acquaintance with spoiled children. "I like paying my own way."

Like a man navigating uncharted waters, Harris carefully changed direction. He seemed determined to do whatever it took to get her into his bed.

"An independent woman? All right, I can respect that." Turning his head, his smile faded. He looked at the server beside the table the way he would have regarded a lower life form. "Well, you heard her. Bring us separate checks."

Alix stopped herself before she could sigh with relief. The evening, she thought, was mercifully going to come to an end.

Or maybe not.

Hunting up her key even before Harris's Ferrari had turned down her block, she tried not to exit the car in a hurry the moment the vehicle came to a stop in her driveway.

Harris was right behind her. She could hear him

chuckling to himself. That could only be a bad thing, she decided.

Shoving the key into the lock, she opened the door, then turned. "Well, good night."

He placed his body in the way, partially blocking her retreat. "Aren't you going to invite me in?"

Only if I can draw and quarter you. She forced a nondescript smile to her lips. She had her excuse ready. "I've got a baby-sitter inside—" It wasn't true. Norma, the eternal grandmother, had elected to take Julie for the night. But there was no way she was about to let Harris know that.

"Sitters can be sent away."

She didn't like the way he treated people, as if they were there solely for his own purposes. "This is Norma, my father's housekeeper. She practically raised me—"

The information had no impact on Harris. The sitter was an obstacle, nothing more. "She's on payroll, send her away."

Alix squared her shoulders. Definitely penance, she thought, regarding Harris. "I don't think so, William."

The expression on his face became nasty. "Look, you can't jerk me around like this."

That tore it. She braced herself for a possible scene. "There was no jerking involved, William." Her voice was stony. "We went out, we had dinner, we paid for dinner and now dinner is over."

He loomed over her, his very body language a threat. "But not the evening."

She looked up at him, not about to be intimidated. "It is for us. I have a headache, remember?"

Giving it one more try, Harris summoned his best seductive manner and leaned in closer to her. "I know how to make it go away."

She never budged. "So do I. Leave." When he made no movement, she added. "Now."

The little tease, he thought. What she needed was to be taught a lesson, and he would have been glad to be the one to do it. But right now, he couldn't risk possible repercussions. Juarez, the man with all the connections, the man who held his life in his hands, had warned him to keep a low profile or suffer the consequences.

Still, he didn't like being played like this. "Or you'll do what?"

Her eyes were steely. She'd played poker ever since she could reach the table. She knew how to bluff effectively. "You don't want to push me, William. You really don't."

Terrance was back where he'd been originally, parked across from her house. Three times, listening to the exchange, he'd begun to leave the car. Three times he'd sunk back down, tense, waiting.

Grudging admiration wove in and out of his mind.

Alix was more than holding her own. To go racing out to defend her, especially since she didn't seem to need it, would definitely tip his hand. She would know that he was out here, hovering protectively. He wasn't sure just what kind of message that would send to her. Or to Harris.

Still, he looked forward to getting into some kind of physical confrontation with the man. Terrance promised himself it would happen.

Primitive, but there you had it, he thought. At bottom there was a little Neanderthal in the best of them.

And then it was over. A very angry-looking Harris turned away from Alix's door and stormed off to his Ferrari. Alix closed her door firmly behind him.

"Best laid plans of mice and men, pal," Terrance murmured under his breath, grinning. He removed his earpiece. There was no need for it now.

Waiting for a decent interval to pass, Terrance started up his car and drove to his apartment. Whistling.

"Where the hell have you been?" Riley wanted to know, emerging out of the shadows the moment he walked up to the front door. "I've been trying to call you for the better part of an hour. Did you fall into a black hole?"

His car keys still in his hand, Terrance was mildly

surprised to find his partner waiting for him. "Cell phones still leave a lot to be desired. I was out doing surveillance on Harris, why?"

Had something gone down? Terrance asked himself. If it had, it had gone down without Harris, which didn't quite make sense, unless they'd been given a bogus tip to begin with. Somehow his gut told him that it didn't seem likely.

About to answer, Riley came to a stop midword. He stared at Terrance.

"Surveillance? Why? The man had a date tonight. With Dr. DuCane." The light dawned even as he uttered the last sentence. A grin spread out over his round face. "Doing a little stalking these days, are we?"

Terrance didn't share in his partner's merriment. "The man is slime. I wanted to be sure Alix was all right."

Riley could appreciate what Terrance was going through. Alix DuCane was a fine looking woman. In Terrance's place, he probably would have done the same thing, though in actuality, it seemed pointless. "Lady looks like she can handle herself."

Stubbornly Terrance pushed on. "He outweighs her by almost a hundred pounds. I thought I'd tip the odds in her favor in case something happened."

"And did it?"

Terrance looked at him seriously. "He tried to push his way into her house."

"And you sprang to the rescue, pure of heart, sound of mind, and proceeded to pummel our best connection to the American side of the Colombian cartel." Riley sighed, dragging his hand through his jet-black hair. "Did she at least fall into your arms?"

"She didn't have to." Turning his back on Riley, Terrance jammed his key into the lock and opened his door. "No pummeling took place. You're right, she can handle herself." He crossed the threshold, leading the way in. "She gave him his walking papers."

Riley didn't bother trying not to laugh. "Leaving you with your tail between your legs?"

Terrance threw his keys down on the side table and shrugged out of his jacket. "She didn't get to see my tail—or any other part of me."

Riley was trying to piece the story together. "She didn't know you were there?"

Terrance shook his head. "No." His tone called for a change of subject. "Now what's this big thing you have to tell me?"

Riley became all business. "We caught a break. One of our men found out that a big shipment of drugs is set to come into the country."

Now they were getting somewhere. Terrance needed to get his mind back on his work and away from a path it couldn't take, anyway. "When?"

The informant had been unable to pinpoint an exact time. "Soon."

Terrance blew out an annoyed breath. "There's no such date on the calendar."

Riley shrugged. He wandered over to the kitchen and its small refrigerator, opening it. Looked like Terrance didn't shop any better than he did. There was beer and a leftover sandwich from a fast-food restaurant.

"It's better than we had before." Taking out a can, Riley closed the refrigerator. "Hey, don't get testy with me because you couldn't play Sir Lancelot. Maybe Harris'll double back and try again."

He hadn't thought of that. Muttering an oath, Terrance grabbed his jacket and his keys. He was out the door before Riley could blink.

"Hey," he called after Terrance, "I was only kidding."

But Terrance was already driving away.

Harris was nowhere to be seen.

Wherever the man was, he had shed his coat and thus the transmitter. There'd been no sound the entire trip back. Terrance had the monitor on high. The uneasiness grew, taking over the interior of the car until he'd entered Alix's street and seen for himself that Harris's car was not in the area.

In all likelihood the man had probably gone to Gallagher's, or someplace similar, and availed himself of more willing companionship than Alix had proven to be. But Terrance knew better than to rule anything out. Just because he wasn't there didn't mean he wasn't coming back. A wounded ego was a fearsome thing with some men.

Terrance resigned himself to settling in for the time being. Glancing at his watch, he gave Harris an hour. He doubted the man would return after midnight.

Crossing his arms before him, he tried to make himself comfortable. He never got the chance to try. Within ten minutes of his arrival, he had company.

"What are you doing out here?"

He'd watched her approach, the long deep-blue robe Alix had on opening and closing about her legs with each step she took toward him. How did the woman manage to get better looking every time he saw her? It didn't seem possible. Or fair.

He gave her his widest, most innocent smile and hoped for the best. "I could tell you that I ran out of gas."

Right in front of her house? Not hardly. She fisted her hands on her hips. "And I could say you were lying. Are you spying on me?"

It amused him that this one time, the truth of the situation would actually work for him, even though he knew she'd probably think he was lying. "No, I'm not. I'm spying on Harris."

He'd developed a knack for twisting words, she

thought. "Is that your way of saying that you've appointed yourself my guardian angel?"

For the moment he rather liked that description. "Something like that."

It had to be a male thing. She didn't appreciate being the bone that two dogs fought over, just on principle. "Well, don't bother, I can take care of myself."

He nodded. The woman was nothing short of magnificent when she was angry. Damn but he'd missed her. "I know, I saw."

Harris had been gone for a good forty-five minutes. She'd just chanced to notice Terrance's car when she went to close her living room drapes. "Just how long have you been out here?"

He shrugged his shoulder. "Long enough."

Obviously, that meant he was here for Harris's less than stellar exit. "Then you saw him go home."

He knew what she was saying—why hadn't he gone home himself. "I know his type. I thought he might come back and try to convince you to reconsider."

She read between the lines. Alix felt her anger slipping away even though she knew she was safer with it. "Flattering though that is, I don't think the man feels I'm the only date in town."

"No, but you obviously weren't dazzled by his charms. That's got to hurt. Especially for a man like Harris who needs constant reassurance."

And he was worried about her. She didn't want to be touched, but she was. "Picked that up, did you?" She crossed her arms before her, regarding him. "You're more intuitive than I thought."

He grinned up at her. "I was always intuitive."

"Not really." It was chilly and she was getting goose bumps that she preferred to attribute to the weather and not the man. Alix glanced over her shoulder toward her house. "Do you want to come in and finish this conversation inside? I don't usually conduct business out in the middle of the street in my robe."

He should be going. He knew that. Instead he got out of the car. "Good habit not to get into."

She pressed her lips together, holding in a smile as she turned to lead the way into the house. She supposed it was rather sweet of him, to be worried about her like this.

Did it mean that he still cared, or was he just being territorial?

No, that had never been his way. He'd never been one to beat his chest.

But it was best not to overanalyze anything, Alix told herself. That way, there wouldn't be any expectations, any disappointments along the way. Whatever happened, happened.

Once inside she led the way into her kitchen. "Can I offer you something? Coffee? Herbal tea? Bottled water?"

What he wanted her to offer was something he wouldn't have been able to accept, anyway. "Water'll be fine. Out of the tap," he told her as she started for the refrigerator.

She filled a glass, then handed it to him as she sat down at the kitchen table opposite him. "What did you think he was going to do, force himself on me?"

"Well, not at the restaurant."

Her eyes widened. "You followed us to the restaurant?" She didn't bother waiting for him to answer. "You know, in some states, they'd call that stalking."

"Like I said—" he set the glass on the table "—it wasn't you I was following. It was Harris."

She raised her brow, amused. Yeah, right. "In some states, they'd call that something else." She stopped being independent and allowed herself just to be female. "Although I suppose I could see your concern. Harris is an odd duck, I can say that for him. One minute he's throwing his weight around, making nurses' lives miserable with his demands, the next I see him off in a corner, palling around with one of the security guards."

About to pick up his glass, he set it down again. He tried not to look more than mildly interested. "Security guard? When?"

"The other day." She stopped, remembering. "Day before yesterday I think. I was going to the cafeteria and I saw Harris talking to this man—definitely not his type.''

He looked at her, trying to follow. ''What's that supposed to mean?''

''The guard looked like one of those types who dragged their knuckles on the ground when they walked. Definitely not in the league William Harris likes to think he's in. The other man could break someone like Harris in two if he wanted to. I can't think of anything they'd have in common.''

But Terrance could.

Chapter 10

He had to get this information Alix had just inadvertently given him to Riley, and the sooner the better.

That meant getting up and going home.

But instead of taking his leave, Terrance heard himself saying, "Mind if I use your bathroom?"

Alix tightened the sash at her waist before answering. "Go right ahead." She directed him to the powder room rather than the full bathroom upstairs. "There's one just to the left of the front door. You passed it on your way here."

He nodded. "I remember. Thanks."

It was hardly more than a large closet, done in light blue and ivory. Once inside the small room,

Terrance closed the door and checked his cell phone. He had a signal. Sometimes, he thought, the planets did align themselves correctly.

He lost no time in contacting Riley.

It took five rings to reach him. Terrance almost hung up when he heard: "Riley."

Terrance wasted no time with a greeting. "Harris has been in contact with one of the security guards at the hospital. He'd need the inside help to smuggle the drugs into Blair."

"McCall?" Riley asked needlessly. "Oh, so now your cell phone's working again." He didn't give Terrance a chance to answer. "Which security guard?"

"I don't have a name, but from the description, it's the big, burly one."

Riley paused. "That could fit about five of them."

Terrance wondered if there was anything he'd forgotten to add. "He was on duty day before yesterday, midday shift."

There was silence again on the other end. "Narrows the playing field a little. Where did you suddenly get this information?"

He knew he was opening up an avenue for Riley, but this was no time to play games. "Alix saw the two of them talking."

"Oh." The word had a very pregnant sound to it. "And just where are you now?"

Terrance blew out a breath, in no mood for any of Riley's ragging. "I'm in her bathroom."

Riley laughed. "I take it that there're no handy phone booths around to change into your superhero costume?"

"Just see what you can find out," Terrance told him impatiently. "Run all their names and prints through the database."

"Aye-aye, Captain. I remember how to do my job, McCall. You just be sure you remember how to do yours."

He didn't ask for an explanation. He knew what Riley was implying. Kidding or not, Terrance didn't appreciate it. He never allowed anything to get in the way of his work, not even a woman whose very presence sent his temperature up a few degrees.

Flipping the phone shut, he tucked it away into his pants pocket. Terrance flushed the toilet and then ran the tap water for good measure, to justify his exit.

It was best if he got going, he thought.

Opening the door, he found Alix standing less than two feet away. She was looking at him oddly, as if trying to figure something out.

"Were you talking to someone in there?"

Hindsight told him that he could have said he was just talking to himself. But he said the first thing that came to mind. "My answering service. Were you listening at the door?"

She lifted one shoulder in a careless shrug. "You were taking a while, I thought maybe there was something wrong." A smile he'd always found engaging curved her mouth. "Occupational habit, I guess."

He looked toward the door. He really should be leaving. Especially since he wanted to stay. Still, his feet insisted on remaining planted where they were. "Yes, but most of the people that you come in contact with in your occupation barely reach your waist."

Again she lifted a single shoulder, dismissing his point. "I can't seem to rein it in." And then she looked at him more closely. "Since when did you get an answering service?"

He was really hoping she wouldn't ask that. Since he had no practice, there was no reason to have a service yet, other than for vanity, and they both knew he wasn't that type. "I signed up for one last week." Before she could say the obvious, he beat her to it. "I guess that was jumping the gun, but I'm hoping to get into a partnership with someone very soon." He lobbed the ball back into her court. "Know any pediatricians who might need to have their workload reduced?"

He meant her, she thought. This time her reaction wasn't an immediate no. This time, just for arguments sake, she turned the idea around in her head. A partnership with Terrance. Sharing the same office space. Seeing each other on a regular, five-days-a-week basis. That would really be playing with fire.

"I'll ask around," she promised noncommittally. "In the meantime, why don't you give me your service number? I might as well have it if I need you."

Damn it, she was asking for the number. That was just what he was afraid of. Trapped, he rattled one off to her, having no idea who she would reach if she used it. He supposed he could always tell her it was a momentary lapse on his part, but he doubted if she'd believe him.

"Hold it, let me write it down." She turned to open the small drawer in the hall side table where she kept a pad and pen.

He needed a way to distract her. Coming up behind her, he placed his hands on her shoulders. He couldn't help thinking how small, how delicate she felt.

"Do you?"

Alix felt herself stiffening. She was acutely aware of the fact that she was wearing only her nightgown beneath her robe.

And that she was alone in the house.

Alone with a man she'd once loved more than life itself. She could feel pulses begin to throb. "Do I what?"

"Need me?"

Terrance turned her around slowly.

Telling himself he was only playing for time—

trying to distract her from copying down a fake phone number—was an excuse so flimsy it vanished. He was caught in his own diversion. Caught in the look that was in her eyes.

Her lips felt dryer than sandpaper. She had no idea how she pushed the words out past them. "You never know. An emergency might come up, your pager might fail, your cell phone signal might not go through…"

She was babbling and she knew it, but she couldn't center herself, couldn't think clearly.

"That's what I always liked about you, Alix, you were always so practical." So beautiful. "Practicality wrapped in femininity."

"But you left, anyway."

Where was her anger? She couldn't summon it, couldn't rouse the emotion that would keep her safe from the look in his eyes, from the overwhelming pull of his body as it stood, less than a hair's breadth away from hers.

It was her only shield, her only defense, and it was gone.

"Everyone makes one major mistake in their lives." He couldn't draw his eyes away from her. Couldn't make himself take the steps he knew he had to, steps that would lead him to the front door, to cool air and sanity. "Leaving you was mine."

She clenched her hands at her sides to keep from trembling. It didn't work. "So now what?"

He ran his hands along her arms, his eyes on hers. "I don't know, Alix. I don't know," he repeated, at a loss. "Play it by ear?"

She felt his hands as they began to slide the robe from her shoulders. A shiver of anticipation zig-zagged through her.

"Those aren't your ears," she murmured.

His smile went straight to her heart, taking no detours, taking no prisoners.

"I'm versatile." He pressed a kiss to the slope of her shoulder and heard her sigh. Excitement drummed through him like a Sousa march.

This was wrong, he thought. All wrong.

This wasn't fair to her and she was the one who mattered in this. She always had been.

Terrance drew his head back and looked at her. How could he walk away again? How could he walk away now? "I haven't heard Julie tonight."

This was her one lifeline, her one way out. She could say something about needing to check on the child and that he should go. He didn't need to know that Julie was peacefully sleeping in her grandfather's house, in the room he had set aside for the little girl.

Tell him. Tell him to go.

But old, familiar sensations were beginning to gather within her, holding a rally, ready to launch into a victory dance. She couldn't bring herself to lie to him, not even to protect herself.

She didn't want to be protected, not tonight.

"That's because Julie's not here. She's at my father's."

Did that mean that she had set the stage earlier for Harris to stay the night? Don't go there, he warned himself. Harris wasn't here. And he was.

He brushed her hair from her face, thinking of the man she'd mentioned. The man he'd always admired. "How is your father?"

She smiled, her stomach quivering as Terrance feathered his fingers along her bare skin. "Still terrific. Still practicing."

He skimmed his lips along the hollow of her throat. "I always liked your father."

Her head fell back, her body quickened. "And he always liked you. It was his one lapse in judgment."

The words were getting harder and harder to utter. He was cutting off her air supply—he and his roaming lips, his roaming hands. They were all conspiring against her, to make her dizzy.

She could feel Terrance's fingers working away at the knot in her sash, even as his mouth gave her no peace.

And then the sash was free, and the robe was parting from her body. Cool air found her, to be instantly replaced with a surge of heat that went through her the moment his hands touched her.

They passed softly, lightly, reverently along her waist, moving upward.

Anticipation warred with common sense, struggling for possession. Her breath caught in her throat.

"Terry..."

She only called him that at her most vulnerable moments. She was his for the taking, he thought, and he wanted to take her more than he wanted to breathe.

Terrance could feel his body almost vibrating with intense longing.

But his ingrained sense of right and wrong insisted on intervening. This was an interlude, just an interlude. He knew that. He'd be gone once the operation was resolved. And even if he wasn't, how would she react to being lied to all this time? To being shut out like some stranger because he couldn't risk telling her the truth? Not because he couldn't trust her—he did, he trusted her with his life. But this didn't involve just him, there were other lives at stake, lives he couldn't hand to her. The wrong word said at the wrong moment could cost them everything. He couldn't burden her with that.

With supreme effort he drew back, cupping her face in his hand and looking at her. "Alix, if—"

No. No, he wasn't going to give her a choice, she thought desperately. He wasn't going to allow her a way out at the last moment. She wouldn't let him, couldn't let him. Everything hummed within her, wanting him. Wanting this.

Before Terrance could say another word, she rose up on her toes, wound her fingers into the folds of his shirt and pulled him to her. She seized his lips with her own, cutting off any last-ditch attempt to spare her. Kissing him as hard as she could.

Despite the anger she'd felt, she always knew Terrance was a good man, a man given to being kind even at his own expense. She didn't want his kindness, she wanted him, his touch, his body. She wanted to remember what it felt like to be completely alive, to be wanted by the only man who had ever truly mattered to her.

The tentacles of desire closing about him, Terrance tightened his arms around Alix, holding her to him, absorbing her frantic heartbeat as his own. Because it was.

His mouth slanted over hers, reveling in what she offered, his body ignited with a fire that refused to be quenched. That hadn't been quenched in all these years. Not since he'd left her.

Alix's robe slid to the floor like an wistful sigh. Terrance struggled to rein himself in. It would have taken so little to shred the nightgown from her body. Instead he coaxed the straps from her shoulders, tugged it away from her breasts down supple hips that begged for his touch.

As he filled his hands with her, the nightgown slowly floated down until it merged with her robe. She was nude, as perfect as he remembered.

More.

Taking a step back, he wrapped her in his gaze. Her waist was still as small as ever, her figure slightly more curved because of the child she'd borne.

He dove his fingers into her hair, framing her face. Wanting her. Somewhere along the perimeter of his mind, a small voice begged him to go slow. Because this would be all he'd have, and it needed to last him the rest of his life.

"Motherhood agrees with you."

Her heart was hammering in her throat so hard, she was sure it was going to pop out at any moment. "You talk too much."

Alix caught his lips between her teeth, suckling for a moment before losing herself in one deep, twelve-story kiss.

Even as her mouth was sealed to his, Terrance could feel Alix working away at his clothes. Two buttons didn't make the journey as she tore his shirt from him. Her hands were trembling as she un-hooked the clasp at his jeans. He was vaguely aware that he came to her aid, undoing them when she fumbled.

Quickly, she slid the denim from his hips and thighs, her hands hot along his body.

He wanted to drive himself into her then and there. It was only by exercising the maximum limit of his restraint that he managed not to.

She deserved better.

They both did.

This was not about satisfying lust, this was about revisiting a place they had once inhabited. This was about returning to a time when they had felt that everything was before them, untainted and pure. When there were answers instead of merely questions.

His clothes in a heap beside hers, Terrance picked her up in his arms. Alix twined her arms around his neck and snuggled against him.

"Where's your bedroom?"

She pointed to the stairs, then smiled. Her eyes were bright with humor and pleasure.

He wanted to share in whatever she was thinking. "What?"

She watched the stairs draw closer. "I always wanted to be Scarlett O'Hara."

Terrance began to climb the stairs, holding her to him. The image pleased him. "As I recall, Scarlett O'Hara had on clothes when Rhett carried her up to their bedroom."

She laughed softly against him. "That was the G-rated version." She could feel her body tingling, priming. Yearning for the last moment, yet wanting to hold it off for as long as possible. Wanting this island of time to go on forever.

"And what version is this?"

Her eyes teased him. "You tell me."

He was at her door then, shouldering it open and bringing her inside. Very gently he laid her on the bed. Less than a heartbeat later, he was beside her. "Maybe we'll go for X."

She raised her arms to him. "Making love with you was always far too beautiful to be rated X."

There was no holding back any longer, no recriminations, no regrets. There was only the two of them, only pleasure.

No one could make her body hum the way he could. He knew all her secret places, knew how to arouse her to the point of climax, only to begin the process again.

She thought her heart would beat its way out of her chest. Like a gifted musician, Terrance strummed his fingers along her body, playing her like a beloved instrument, too long kept in storage.

She wound her fingers into her comforter, arching against Terrance, against his mouth as it followed a path forged by his fingers seconds earlier.

Crying out his name, panting, Alix used the last bit of her strength to reverse their positions until she was the one on top.

"Now what?" he asked, surprised, his hands about her hips.

"Now I torture you."

"This isn't torture."

"Wait," she promised, beginning.

Laughter in her eyes, she teased him with her

body, sliding it along his, nibbling here, sampling there, until she was filled with his dark tastes. The laughter faded as she became caught in her own trap, bringing them both up to the point of no return.

Satisfied that he couldn't hold back any longer, she straddled his hips, fitting her legs around him. Her eyes on his face, she drew him into her.

It took everything she had not to lose herself in the moment. Instead, concentrating, Alix began to move ever so slowly.

But the pace quickened almost instantly as his hips rose in response.

"C'mere," Terrance coaxed, his voice a harsh whisper as he reached for her.

She couldn't have denied him if she'd wanted to. And she didn't want to.

Never breaking the ever increasing rhythm, Alix spread her body over his, covering it, their hot flesh mingling and searing each other as they moved faster and faster to a destination they could no longer humanly keep at bay.

"Oh, Terry, I've missed you," she cried as she felt the explosion take hold of her.

She knew by his reaction that she wasn't alone. That he had gone the distance with her. Terrance caught her mouth with his and kissed her so deeply, she didn't think she would ever surface again.

It really didn't matter to her if she didn't. This was where she wanted to be.

Forever.

Chapter 11

"You know, I didn't come over for this."

Terrance wasn't sure just where he found the strength to tuck his arm around Alix and draw her to him, but he did. It was the wee hours of the night and they were still awake. Part of that was because they'd made love two more times, each time being more erotic than the last.

The marathon brought back happier days, and he hadn't wanted to close his eyes and risk discovering that all of this had been just a dream. A wonderful, passionate dream.

Alix turned toward him, her hair tickling his cheek. Longing made a return appearance. He wondered if there was some Guinness world record that covered this sort of thing.

"As I remember it." Alix skimmed her finger over his lips, her eyes teasing his. "I was the one who invited you in, not the other way around."

Catching her hand, he pressed a kiss to her palm and succeeded in arousing both of them. "Did you think we were going to wind up like this?"

She laughed softly. The ghost of better times hovered around in her brain. "There was a time that we *always* wound up like this." And then, because she didn't want him getting the wrong idea about her reaction to tonight, she added quickly, "Oh, don't worry. I'm not digging out old wedding invitations."

He raised his head to look at her face. "You had wedding invitations?"

Damn, how had she let that slip out? "Just one package." Her tone was dismissive. "I got it in a stationery store, one of those do-it-yourself deals for the computer." And then, because this was Terrance and she'd never lied to him, she confessed, "I just wanted to know what it would look like, seeing your name and mine linked in something official."

Guilt galloped up on a white charger, holding a lance aimed straight at his conscience.

"Oh, God, Alix—"

Something stirred within her. "That wasn't said to make you feel guilty, that was just sharing something. The bottom line is that there's no pressure here, okay?" She tucked the sheet more tightly around her breasts. "I don't expect either one of us to pick up where we left off. A lot's happened since then."

She didn't know the half of it, Terrance thought, feeling another stab of guilt.

"I've had a life," Alix was saying. "So have you. You've undergone changes."

A look she couldn't quite read crossed his face. It nudged at her curiosity, just the way seeing him with Harris on more than several occasions did. He'd made it clear earlier tonight that he thought of Harris as lowlife, yet he had spent time with him. It didn't add up. Just like seeing him hang up abruptly the other day when he saw her approaching didn't make sense.

Granted she might be making a mountain out of a handful of Play-Doh. But she couldn't shake free of the thought that these small instances of behavior, and others like them, didn't quite ring true, didn't seem in character for the man she'd once known.

Just how much had he really changed in six years? And changed how, for the worse? She didn't want to think so, but there were times...

There was something in her voice that alerted the agent in him. "Changes?" he echoed. "What kind of changes?"

For a moment, despite the fact that they had just made love for the third time, that they were still lying here, nude beneath the sheets, their bodies touching and damp from the sweat of desire, she felt estranged from him. Adrift on an ocean of loneliness.

She shrugged. "Changes. Like your body's harder now than it was before."

Good, she wasn't alluding to anything more serious. For a second he'd thought she saw through his cover. There were times he could swear she could see right into his mind.

Terrance pretended to glance down past his waist. "Well, that's your work."

She laughed despite the serious bent her thoughts had taken. "I mean your body's harder now than it was six years ago."

He got comfortable again, pulling her to him so that she was on top, her hair a silky blond curtain framing his face on either side. He began to strum his fingers along her body, gently tugging away the sheet.

"I was thinking of something a little more recent." Raising his head, he caught her lower lip and slid his tongue over it ever so lightly.

She could feel her body quickening. Again. She laughed, the sound softly raining down on him. "Your stamina's improved, too."

He grinned and it was positively wicked, so reminiscent of the boy she'd fallen in love with a lifetime ago. He cupped the back of her head, about to guide her mouth down to his. "Like the man said, 'Lady, you ain't seen nothin' yet.'"

"Show me," she whispered, her breath warming his face.

One last time, she thought, just one last time she wanted to lose herself. For it was in the world Terrance created for her in his arms that everything seemed right.

But just as his mouth met hers, the phone beside her bed rang, its shrill noise cracking apart the warmth that had begun to reclaim her.

Already resigned to the inevitable, Alix sighed, sagging against him. She looked accusingly at the phone as it rang again. "You don't think it might be a telemarketer, do you?"

He shook his head, his hands on her slim shoulders. "Not at this time of night."

Blowing out another breath, Alix braced herself. She dragged her body away from his, one last surge of desire shooting through her. Reaching for the telephone, she brought the receiver to her ear.

"Alix DuCane."

He watched her become instantly alert, the wild, unbridled passion vanishing from her countenance as if it had never existed. She sat up, murmuring "Yes, I see. All right." He didn't need to hear the other side of the conversation to know what was going on. She was all pediatrician now, and one of her small patients obviously needed her.

"Take her to Blair's E.R. I'll meet you there in twenty minutes. She'll be fine, Mrs. Lewis. Just keep Claire in a sitting position and get her to the hospital." The instant Alix hung up, she bounced out of bed, making a beeline for her bureau and a fresh set of underwear.

There was nothing to do but get up himself. "Need someone to drive you?" He looked around, trying to remember where he'd left his clothes.

She tried not to look at him. Seeing him naked like that, even after the night they'd spent together, would only make her knees melt and distract her. The man had a body that could bring a stone statue to life.

"No, that's all right," she assured him, turning away. "I have no idea how long I'll be. You go on home. One of us should get a good night's sleep."

He stopped at the doorway, looking for all the world like something Michelangelo would have wanted to preserve for all time. He winked at her.

"I don't think I'll be doing much sleeping," he confided.

She flushed with pleasure, knowing it was adolescent to feel this way. It had been a long time since she'd been an adolescent. And a long time since she'd felt like this, period.

She pulled on a pair of pants and reached for a fresh bra from the drawer.

"You can stay here as long as you'd like, you

know. Julie's at my father's for the night and no-body'll be here until at least midmorning. Norma has no reason to come early with Julie not here. If you're tired—'' She didn't want him driving if he was sleepy.

But he shook his head. "You make me feel like a kept man."

"Very funny." Pulling a blue sweater out of the closet, she quickly donned it. Poking out her head, she saw that he'd left the room. Probably on his way downstairs to his clothes. Thank heaven. "There hasn't been a woman born who could keep you under lock and key," she called after him.

Already downstairs, he paused as he tugged up his jeans. It amazed Terrance how little she knew about the power she had over him. After punching his arms through the shirt, he began buttoning it. There were two buttons unaccounted for in the middle. By all rights, her ignorance should have been a good thing, he thought, but he couldn't make up his mind whether he believed it or not.

"Sure I can't drive you?" he asked as he watched her come flying down the stairs. He pushed his feet into his loafers.

She came to a halt, looking around for her purse. It was under the table. She didn't bother trying to remember how it got there. "I'm sure."

"By the way, what's the emergency?" He

wanted to know. In all the excitement, he'd forgotten to ask.

Catching her hair with one hand, she stuck a barrette through it, keeping it from her face. She looked all of twenty, he thought. "Three-year-old with the croup."

"Scary thing," he agreed.

She remembered her first encounter with the disease that hopscotched through early childhood, wantonly making patients uncomfortable and terrorizing parents. "Scarier looking than it actually is. All parents think their child is choking to death."

About to dash out the door, Alix paused suddenly. Turning toward Terrance, she allowed herself one last quick, hard kiss, knowing that there was nothing about the future she could predict. For all she knew, this was their last kiss and she wanted to leave a resounding impression on him.

"I'll see you at the hospital."

And with that she was gone.

She sank down on the sofa in the doctors' lounge. Her back was killing her, she realized. She couldn't help wondering if that was because she'd been on her feet the last few hours, or because of the acrobatics she'd executed before that.

Didn't matter, it still hurt. And her eyes felt like lead, but she knew that, too, would pass.

As soon as she had the little Lewis girl stabilized,

she'd called her father and explained the situation. She didn't know what time she could come by in the morning to pick Julie up. He'd told her not to worry, that Norma would be more than happy to bring her after breakfast. His housekeeper doted on the little girl as if she were her very own grand-daughter.

At least she didn't have to worry about Julie, Alix thought. Just about everything else.

Her eyes closed, Alix blew out a long breath, wondering if it was the lack of sleep or the evening itself that had her feeling neither here nor there. Well, the evening had accomplished one thing: she'd found out that she still loved Terrance with a fierceness that shook her very soul.

Big surprise there, she mocked herself. In her heart, she'd always known that with very little prod-ding, she would do exactly what she'd done tonight.

Last night, she amended, glancing at her watch. It was almost six in the morning.

So much for playing hard to get, she thought cyn-ically.

But then, she'd never been good at playing any kind of game. Besides, that wasn't the problem right now, anyway. The problem was that she had an un-easy feeling that Terrance was only passing through again. Maybe he'd returned to convince himself that he hadn't made a mistake all those years ago by leaving.

There was something about him, something that she couldn't quite put her finger on. He was edgy, as if he was prepared to vanish at a moment's notice.

You're tired, she told herself.

Tired, and her mind was wandering. This wasn't the time to try to make any life-altering decisions. For now, she decided, life would go on as it had. One day at a time, that was all any of them could live. Done right, the day that followed would take care of itself.

But how did she know what right was?

Alix placed her hand to her forehead. She had a headache and it was only threatening to become worse.

"Coffee helps to open up the capillaries if you have a headache."

Her eyes flew open at the sound of his voice.

Terrance was standing in front of her, holding out a container of coffee like a silent peace offering of some sort. He had a second one in his other hand. Both containers sported the logo of the café across the street. Was it open already? she wondered.

Taking the container from him, she smiled her thanks. "What are you doing here, Terrance? You're not on until eight."

"I thought you might need some decent coffee."

She removed the lid, looking at him incredulously. "So you came in two hours early to bring it to me?"

He dropped into the seat beside her. The chocolate-colored sofa sighed, its cushions sinking and bringing their two bodies closer.

"Seemed like the thing to do." He took a sip of his coffee. "So, how did it go?"

The frantic couple had arrived at the exact same moment she had. "Had more trouble calming down the parents than treating the child." At one point she'd seriously considered giving the mother a sedative.

"First timers?" She nodded in response. "They'll learn." He looked at her. She looked tired clear down to the bone. "If you want to take a quick catnap, I can cover for you."

A fond feeling surged through her. Did that seem like old times or what? Fresh out of medical school, they had both managed to get accepted at the same hospital for their intern stint and had somehow gotten into the same rotation together. During graveyard shift, they would cover for each other when things got slow, with one of them taking on double duty while the other slept for an hour.

And then he'd left.

Somehow, that always seemed to come up out of nowhere, to hit her as hard as it could right between the eyes. But she had to remember that. Because if

she didn't, when he did it again it would be un-
bearable.

Fool me once, shame on you. Fool me twice,
shame on me.

Alix forced a smile to her lips and shook her
head. "No, that won't be necessary. This coffee
should keep me going for a few hours on the fumes
alone. What's in this, anyway? I'm feeling almost
human already."

"Just a double cappuccino." He remembered she
liked regular coffee, but that didn't seem good
enough for the situation. "I took a chance."

She looked at him over the rim of her container.
"Wasn't that much of a chance." She looked at him
significantly, her mind not on the coffee but the
night they'd just shared. "You were pretty assured
of the results."

His smile was slow, easy. "Not as sure as you
might think."

She searched his face. Had he changed that
much? "Never knew you not to be confident."

The shrug was light, careless, belying the import
of the words behind it. "I didn't always tell you
everything."

"No," she agreed, otherwise she would have had
some clue about his sudden departure, been somehow prepared. "You didn't."

But the idea of a Terrance who wasn't sure of his
every move was utterly foreign to her.

Uncertainty shimmered in the air, making her wonder. Was he telling her everything now, or were there things he was keeping back? It suddenly occurred to her that he hadn't done much talking about his life in Boston. Or for that matter mentioned his life once he'd left here. Why? Was he hiding something? A girlfriend? An ex-wife? Or something else?

Trying not to seem too invasive, she turned to face him. "So tell me everything now."

The request took him completely by surprise. He wondered if she was just talking, or if he should read something into it. "Looking for something to put you to sleep?"

"Nothing about you ever put me to sleep, Terrance." The wariness that came into his eyes just made her wonder that much more. Was he protecting secrets?

Damn, reality was a bitter brew to drink. She liked it far better when she believed that Terrance would never lie to her, never hold anything back. When she could believe in him even more than she could believe in herself. But those days were gone.

"Don't look so uneasy, I'm not asking you to play Truth or Dare." She tossed her hair over her shoulder, telling herself she was a big girl now and this kind of thing shouldn't bother her. Losing your dreams, your faith, was all part of being an adult.

"You can keep your secrets. You don't owe me anything."

He wasn't entirely sure what had just happened here, other than he had somehow managed to hurt her again. "Alix—"

Alix rose to her feet, handing him the half-full container and pulling her dignity to her. If she couldn't have his trust or the truth from him, then she didn't want anything from him at all.

"Thanks for the coffee, Terrance. But I just remembered, I'm not on E.R. rotation today. That means I get to go home for that catnap." She glanced at her watch. It was later than she thought. Maybe it was later than they both thought. "I've still got a little less than three hours before I see my first patient."

According to Beauchamp, she still had a few days to go as his E.R. guide and mentor.

"You mean you're letting me fly solo?" Terrance asked.

His light tone left her cold. "As I recall, you tried out your wings a long time ago. They worked just fine." And then, just in case he ran into a problem, she added, "Lukas Graywolf is on if you find yourself running into trouble. And you won't even have to spend the night with him."

He was on his feet beside her. "Alix—"

But she was already turning on her heel and walking away.

He watched her leave, stunned. He wasn't sure what the hell had just happened, but he knew he wasn't happy about it.

"One cold fish, that one." Harris was slurring his words and swaying dangerously on the bar stool that evening. The man had corralled Terrance just before his shift was over, asking him to come to Gallagher's with him. It was obvious Harris wanted to unload to someone, and Terrance had hoped that somewhere in the middle of complaining, the man would let something slip.

No such luck. So far his complaints all centered on Alix and the unfruitful evening Harris and his ego had endured.

He'd been lending a sympathetic ear for the past three hours and he'd had about all he could take of this waste of human flesh, but he bit his tongue. Terrance eyed the way Harris was swaying.

He pointed to a booth in the corner. "Why don't we get a table?"

Harris wrapped both hands around his drink, as if that could somehow steady him. It didn't. "Can't. Need to be out in the thick of things." He nodded at the area around the bar. "Otherwise, how're all these beautiful women going to see me?"

They saw him, all right, Terrance thought. And probably to a one, they were repulsed. He looked down at the ground beneath the stool. "It's long way down to the floor from up there."

Harris tried to stiffen and succeeded marginally. "I've got great balance." He took another partial hit from his glass, then added, "Unlike Juarez."

Terrance pretended not to be familiar with the name. Riley had given him a complete list just this morning before he'd come in to get his head chewed up by Alix. That's what he got for trying to be nice.

"Juarez?"

"Security guard." And then Harris began to laugh as if he'd just told himself a great joke.

"What's so funny?"

"Nothing." Harris began to wave away the question and almost fell from his perch. Terrance caught his arm, steadying him. "You wouldn't understand."

His hand still on Harris's arm, Terrance leaned into him. "Try me."

Harris licked his lips. "Hiring Juarez as a security guard's like getting a wolf to guard the sheep."

Terrance felt he could safely make the only logical guess. He doubted that Harris knew about Juarez's arrests for petty theft. "He takes things?"

Harris looked at him long and hard, as if debating saying something curt. The next minute he burst out laughing. "Like there's Krazy Glue on his fingers."

He and Riley were pretty sure that Juarez had been the guard Alix had seen Harris talking to. But all that could still mean nothing, even with Juarez's rap sheet. It was ancient history and circumstantial. They needed more. "Big things or little things?"

Harris pulled himself up, sitting straighter. "You ask an awful lot of questions."

Terrance shrugged, pretending not to care. "You brought up the subject."

"And since it's my subject, I'm taking it off the table." Using his almost empty glass, he pointed toward two women at the far end of the bar. "Hey, how about those two? You like those two, Terry? I'll let you have first pick."

"They might have something to say about that."

"Yeah. 'Yes,'" Harris said in a breathless voice, mimicking a woman. And then he suddenly paled, his eyes widening in surprise. "Oh, God, I think I'm going to be sick."

Considering how much Harris had imbibed over the course of the past few hours, Terrance was surprised the man hadn't gotten sick sooner.

"Up you go," he said briskly, helping Harris off the stool and to his feet.

Harris turned a shade of green. Moving swiftly, Terrance aimed him toward the men's room, hoping they'd make it before the bartender wound up with something extra to clean up.

With any luck, he figured the two women would be gone by the time he brought Harris out again.

This getting information by inches was a torture, he thought. He carefully pushed Harris into the rest room ahead of him. But it was the very slowness of completing his mission that kept him here, that kept him around Alix.

Folding his arms before him as he stood outside the stall, Terrance waited. There was an up side to everything, he told himself, listening to Harris retch, purging the last three hours worth of drinking.

Even this.

Chapter 12

Slipping on her suit jacket, Alix hurried to her front door. She answered the doorbell on the second ring, throwing it open and uttering a cheery, "Hi, Norma," only to stop short.

It wasn't the gray-haired, full-figured, sweet-faced housekeeper standing on her doorstep, but her father. His right hand was firmly wrapped around his granddaughter's left. The latter gave the impression of a rocket about to be deployed.

"Dad, what are you doing here?"

Daniel DuCane allowed himself to be dragged into the living room by his energized granddaughter. "Playing hooky, just like you."

Alix shut the door. "Hi, pumpkin." She bent

down to kiss her daughter, then rose again, stretching to plant a kiss on her father's cheek.

"I'm not playing hooky, Dad, I'm going to work." She looked down dubiously at her daughter, who had rushed off to the far side of the living room to root through her toy box. "Or, at least, I was."

Daniel strode into the room and made himself comfortable on the sofa. He beamed at Julie. "Don't worry, go ahead." Glancing toward Alix, he knew what his daughter was thinking. It never ceased to amaze him how the younger generation thought they had a monopoly on competence. "Norma'll be here shortly."

Alix shifted uncomfortably, aware how delicate some feelings could be.

"Dad, I didn't mean to imply—"

He laughed. "Sure you did. You think I can't handle a short person." He gave his daughter a scrutinizing look. "Handled you well enough, didn't I, kiddo?"

She couldn't have had a better father if she'd filled out a requisition form and delivered it to God herself. "You handled me just fine, Dad," Alix told him, laying a hand fondly on his shoulder. "I just thought that Julie might be too much for you."

"Not yet." He took out a small, rectangular box from his jacket. It was time to teach his granddaughter dominos. Setting the box on the table, he opened it and dumped out the pieces on the coffee table.

Julie watched his every move, fascinated. "I'll let you know when that happens."

"No, you wouldn't," she said knowingly. "Your pride won't let you."

"Pride's a funny thing." He began laying the dominos facedown one by one. "It can boost you up, help you accomplish things you didn't think you could—" Daniel raised his eyes and looked pointedly at his daughter. She'd been very closemouthed about Terrance the couple of times he'd tried to steer the conversation that way. Normally, they shared everything. "It can also get in your way and keep you from things that it shouldn't."

She leaned over his shoulder and flipped over a domino he'd missed. "Not subtle, Dad, not subtle at all."

For a moment he forgot about the game he wanted to teach Julie. Turning, he gave Alix his full attention. "Hey, I'm an old country doctor, not one of those new, cutting-edge psychiatrists."

"Country doctor, my foot," Alix hooted. "The L.A. basin hasn't been thought of as 'country' for over fifty years."

He gave a careless shrug. "Poetic license. I still feel like a country doctor. Don't forget, when I started practicing, we were still called family doctors, not 'primary care physicians.'" He made no secret that he despised the term. It sounded so distant, so devoid of feeling and everything that he felt a doctor was supposed to stand for. "If that don't make you shiver from the cold, nothing will." He looked at his granddaughter, who had flipped over a domino and was probing the white indentations with tentative fingers. "Right, Julie?"

The little girl looked up at the man adoringly and nodded her head, her baby-fine blond curls bobbing fiercely.

The scene nudged something in Alix's memory. She could remember looking up at her father just that way. To her, he'd seemed ten feet tall and bulletproof back in those days. Now she found herself worrying about him, about his health, about what he ate and if he was getting enough exercise. She missed the old days, she thought wistfully.

"Anyway, I won't be distracted," Daniel informed her. He pinned her with a look. "Talked to Terrance lately?"

She began looking around for her purse. She was sure she left it here somewhere. "I'm his 'guide,' I talk to him all the time."

With all the pieces facedown, he began to move them around, mixing them up. "Don't play coy with me, Al, you know what I'm asking."

"Yes, I know what you're asking." She debated ending it there. But because he meant well, she admitted, "A little."

"Good." He nodded. "Dialogue is good. But?"

Alix raised a brow quizzically. "There's a 'but' on your face."

Finding her purse, she slipped the straps on her shoulder. "Sounds anatomically improbable, or at the very least, horribly uncomfortable."

"Make jokes. I'll be here when you need to talk."

She kissed his cheek again, grateful that he understood. "I know that, Dad, and I appreciate it. But some things I just have to sort out myself."

Daniel sighed, then nodded. "Toughest part of being a parent."

"What is?" She paused, curious.

"Staying on the outside when you want to go rushing in, making everything better," her father said.

Alix knew there'd been a time when she'd come to him with everything and he had been able to make it right. But that had been before puberty had hit.

"Wait, your turn'll come," he added, then looked at the little girl who was eyeing the domino pieces with unabashed curiosity. "Right Julie?"

"Right," she echoed.

"Go." Daniel waved his daughter toward the door. "Uphold the DuCane name." He glanced at the clock on the mantel. "Can't have you coming in late."

"I'll see you later, Dad." Alix pulled open the front door. "Norma is coming, right?"

"Yes, Norma's coming." Hearing a car approaching, he leaned back in his seat and was able to partially see out the front door. "See, there she is, pulling up in the driveway now." His eyes met Alix's. "I'm not an old man, Alix."

"Sure you are," she only half teased. "You're my old man—" she flashed him a smile "—and I want to keep you around forever and ever."

"Being with Julie keeps me young." Making a decision, he rose. The dominos would keep until later. He put his hand out to his granddaughter. "Let's go play on the slide, honey."

"Dad!"

He raised his hand in a solemn promise. "I'll be the one with my feet on the ground." And then he winked at her just before he left with Julie.

Alix shook her head as she hurried out. Just her luck, she had to have Peter Pan as a father. She nodded a greeting to Norma as she past the woman.

She was going to be late if even one light in her path was red.

Something wasn't quite right, wasn't quite in sync. Alix couldn't shake the feeling, hadn't been able to, almost since the first. Terrance was hiding something.

Was there someone back in Boston, someone he

hadn't told her about? Someone who loved him the way she had? It would go a long way to explaining the couple of times he'd abruptly ended phone conversations when she came on the scene.

She'd been semipreoccupied all morning, allowing extraneous thoughts to infiltrate her mind when she should have been thinking about her patients.

There wasn't going to be any peace until she sorted things out for herself, she knew that. But how? She couldn't ask Terrance about it, not yet at any rate, because if she was wrong, he'd think she was paranoid.

She wasn't wrong. She knew him too well. Something was up.

The best way, she decided as she made her final notations on the Gomez baby's chart, was to start at the beginning. In this case, that meant Boston General.

She dropped off the file on her nurse's desk and entered the next room, issuing a greeting to the parents and child there.

She'd become friendly with a doctor at a convention she'd attended two years ago. The woman was a young widow, too. They'd shared a few meals, stories and swapped sympathies. Stephanie Geller was based at Boston General.

Maybe if she asked Stephanie a few questions…

It was a comforting thought. "Okay, let's see what you weigh, shall we?" Alix said cheerfully to the little boy who was exactly six months older than her daughter.

Alix waited until her lunch break and then looked up Stephanie Geller's number. It took a little maneuvering to get past the woman's receptionist.

"Hi, Stephanie, this is Alix DuCane."

"Alix, what a nice surprise. Are you in the city?"

Alix rocked back in her chair, looking out the window. It was a clear day, and from where she sat, she could see Catalina.

"No, still on the West Coast." She felt a little guilty, calling out of the blue like this solely to ask for a favor. It had been a while.

"Must be nice. The weather's awful here. It's been snowing off and on for three days now. So tell me, what can I do for you? Is this an official call?"

She knew the other woman was asking if she was calling for a consultation. "This isn't exactly about a patient. It's about a doctor."

"Oh?" There was a significant pause on the other end as Stephanie considered the options. "Someone stirring your heart?"

Was she that transparent?

"What makes you ask that?"

"There's a funny note in your voice." When they'd last talked, there had been no one in Alix's life. Stephanie had felt bad because she had just started seeing someone and was convinced she was in love. She wanted that kind of good feeling for Alix, too. "So, tell me all about him."

"That's just it." Alix hesitated, then forged on. "I was hoping you could do that for me."

"Come again?"

Maybe this was a bad idea, Alix thought. Maybe she wouldn't like what she heard. *Too late now, you put your foot into it.*

She had no choice but to continue. "He just transferred from Boston General's pediatric department a month ago. I thought that maybe you knew him."

"I'm in ob-gyn," Stephanie reminded her. "But we do intersect. What's his name?"

Alix took a deep breath. It was like diving into an icy lake. "Terrance McCall."

"Sorry, name doesn't ring a bell."

Alix felt a sinking sensation in the pit of her stomach. "You sure?"

"Describe him."

"Six-one, dirty-blond hair. Muscular. Deep-blue eyes. Thirty-six."

"Wow, sounds yummy, but nope, nobody I know." There was a touch of regret in Stephanie's voice. "But, hey, this is a big hospital. There are a lot of doctors on staff I don't know by name. My time has gotten rather limited since I've started seeing Adam." She stopped before she went off on a tangent. "Do you think this Terrance is lying to you?"

"No—" That wasn't strictly true, Alix thought. "I don't know."

"Tell you what, first chance I get, I'll see if I can find someone in administration to do a search for me on the database. That make you feel better?"

"Actually, no," Alix confessed. Her stomach rumbled, reminding her that she'd slept through the time she'd allotted herself for breakfast. "I feel like I'm snooping."

"You are, but hey, this day and age, it pays to be careful."

She knew that, Alix thought several minutes later as she hung up the receiver. Trouble was, she didn't really want to be. Not when it came to Terrance.

But she had to be. *Especially* when it came to Terrance, she told herself. He was the one who'd hurt her before.

He couldn't hurt her if she didn't let him, she insisted silently. If she hardened her heart and just concentrated on having nothing more than a good time.

Too late, a voice whispered in her head. Stubbornly she shut it out.

It was coming together. Bit by bit the operation was being pieced together like a giant patchwork quilt. Information trickled in from a variety of sources, wiretaps, snitches and just plain hard detective work. The parts only making sense when fit into the whole.

Because of one late-night cell phone call, they had discovered that the security guard unlocked the basement doors for the laundry trucks twice a week. Tuesdays to collect the dirty hospital laundry, Fridays to leave clean laundry in their place. Riley had gone on to find out that because of cost cuts, a new laundry service was handling Blair's laundry. They had only been doing business with the hospital for the past year.

The company was owned by a holding company which in turn was connected to one of the owners of the casino that Harris frequented. A casino where he had dropped large sums of money on a fairly regular basis. An earlier investigation had turned up that Harris was heavily in debt to the casino. He had exhausted the trust fund left to him by his mother and had tapped out every source of money and then some. He was a man with his back against the wall. And then the casino boss had given him a way out. All they needed was a place to deposit the drugs when they arrived in the country until the heat was off.

The drugs were hidden in the laundry baskets.

Now all that was left was to wait for a shipment and catch everyone involved red-handed.

Waiting was the hardest part of what he did. He

didn't have Monroe's knack for it. Waiting frayed nerves that were already thin.

Even if waiting had been a piece of cake for him, having Alix as the wild card in all this unsettled everything. Terrance was having a hard time keeping his mind on the operation, especially when all he could think about was sleeping with her again.

He knew, when Alix had all but picked a fight the day after they had made love, that he should leave it alone. That it was best all around to let the situation just slide until it was firmly nestled in the past, the way the rest of their history was.

Terrance had a hundred arguments for why he shouldn't be doing this, shouldn't be driving to her place after his shift at the hospital was over.

He was asking for trouble, pure and simple. Alix could be out with another man. She could have decided to shoot first and ask questions later when he turned up on her doorstep. He could be compromising, if not the operation, at least his own part in it. He was blunting his edge.

The list went on and on.

None of it mattered. Not when his every waking thought centered on the fact that he just wanted to see her again. See her the way he couldn't see her in the hospital.

Arriving in her driveway, he jumped out of the car and purposefully strode toward the door. He rang the bell and waited, then rang it again, wondering if this was a huge, huge mistake on his part.

Maybe she wasn't home.

The lights were on, but that didn't mean anything. They could have been left on, or turned on automatically to make it look as if there was someone home. He was the first to know about facades.

After the third ring he gave up, telling himself it was a sign intended for him to get his mind back on his work and not on the woman who could have been his wife, had things gone differently.

About to turn away, he heard the door opening behind him.

The last time he'd been outside her door, she'd had on a robe. This time she was wearing a large white bath towel tucked around her body. There were droplets of water still clinging to her shoulders and a look of less than patience on her face.

"Yes?"

"You shouldn't answer the door like that." She was shivering. He invited himself in just to get her out of the open. Inside, he turned around to look at her, unable to help himself. "That's taxing a man's self-restraint."

She shut the door and glared at him. "I was taking a bath." *Trying to get you off my mind.* "Besides, I looked through the peephole." *Damn it, she should have grabbed her robe instead of just a towel,* but she'd forgotten to take a robe in with her. She sighed, frustrated, unsettled. "Why are you here?"

He sank his hands into his pockets to keep them away from the edge of her towel. "I didn't like the way we left things the other day."

She put space between them. "I think the operating word here is *left*. Maybe we should." Maybe it was the only way she'd find any peace. If she separated herself from him. "Maybe we should just leave things as they are."

"In chaos?" He didn't want to leave things the way they were. He'd tried that, tried keeping his distance and it wasn't working.

She drew herself up, deliberately making her voice distant, her eyes cold. "It's been done before."

"All right." He put his hand on the doorknob. He wasn't going to beg. But then something within him rebelled. Dropping his hand to his side, he swung around. "No, damn it. I don't want to leave things the way they are."

She stared at him. So what was he saying? That he wanted to begin again?

Continue the way things had been going?

Have a private place where he could come by and have a quickie?

No, that wasn't strictly true, she amended. The anger she was vainly attempting to gather to her was falling by the wayside. There'd been nothing quick about the evening they'd shared last week. Or any of the other evenings that lived on in the past they'd once shared.

But she didn't know if she was up to getting back into the front car of the roller coaster to go plunging down steep inclines again. For a long moment, her arms crossed before her, she studied him, trying to block out the feelings that were tiptoeing around her, attempting to break in.

"My friend doesn't remember you."

Out of left field, the statement threw him completely. Who was she talking about? "What?"

She watched his face intently. Could she tell if he was lying? She wanted to believe that she could but she wasn't sure anymore. "A woman I know on the staff of Boston Memorial, Dr. Stephanie Geller, she doesn't remember you."

His eyes narrowed. "Are you checking up on me?"

"You're changing the subject."

"That *is* the subject." He stood, looking down at her, searching her eyes. The business he was in had made him paranoid. He tried to remind himself that this was Alix, that she wasn't a part of his operation, except in the most peripheral of ways. "Why are you checking up on me, Alix?"

He had to ask? The old Terrance would have known. "Because things aren't adding up. Because you're palling around with William Harris—"

"You went out with him," he was quick to counter.

"He was persistent and I was trying to forget about you—" She saw Terrance opening his mouth. "And if you tell me you're hanging around him to forget about me, I swear I'll hit you."

Inadvertently she had just handed him his excuse. "Then get ready to swing." Terrance looked at her innocently.

"Why?" Feeling her towel loosen, she tucked it in against her breasts. She wasn't buying any of this. "So you work both sides of the street now?"

"No, but when he goes out, he only has one objective, to get lucky."

"So that's why you're with him? To 'get lucky'?" she cried contemptuously.

She began to turn away, but he caught her by the shoulders, forcing her to look at him. "So far I haven't been. I can't seem to forget about you."

Oh no, he wasn't going to look at her with those soulful eyes, he wasn't going to wiggle out of everything he'd done that easily. There was a lot for him to account for. "So what happened for those six years? You had amnesia?"

He was tired of dancing around, tired of trying to second-guess her and divert her. Though he had no right to her, all he wanted was to have her in his life.

"How many ways do I have to apologize for that?"

"I don't know," she told him honestly. "Until I can learn to trust you again. Once trust is gone, it's not a simple matter to get it back."

"My father died, the field I put my heart and soul into couldn't save him. It felt as if everything I believed in was a lie."

She fought back the tears that stung her eyes. She hated the fact that she started to cry when she got angry. "I wasn't a lie. I would have been there for you no matter what. We loved each other, you were supposed to turn to me when you were having a crisis, not limp into some out-of-the-way cave like a wounded bear," she insisted hotly, her temper flaring. "This wasn't about survival of the fittest, this was about love."

He shrugged helplessly. "I didn't want to bring you down."

Of all the stupid—

"Oh, and suddenly finding myself with only half my heart, half my life, that wasn't supposed to bring me down?" She had to curb herself to keep from shouting at him.

He could only offer her the truth now and hope that she would understand. "I had to find myself."

She looked at him, her battle against the tears lost as she remembered the pain, the sorrow. Remembered everything.

"Why did you have to lose me to do it?"

Chapter 13

Terrance leaned his forehead against hers.

"Alix, I only know that losing you was the worst thing I could have done."

And it was the truth. He wasn't sorry about the turns his life had taken, only that they hadn't included her.

But now he was so entrenched in this life he was living, in this lie he'd had to weave, that he didn't think he could ever work his way out. Ever get back to where he had once been. Much as he wanted to, he didn't see her forgiving him for lying to her again.

Terrance sighed, squaring his shoulders. His being here was only torturing both of them. "Maybe I'd better go."

Turning away from her, he crossed to the door. His hand was on the doorknob when he heard Alix softly say, "Maybe you'd better stay."

Surprised, he looked at her over his shoulder. "If I stay..." He let his voice trail off.

He didn't have to say it. "I know." Alix remained where she was standing, waiting for him to make the next move. Knowing she was playing with fire, but there was no way around it. She was going to get burned if he left again, one way or another. She might as well let him stay for as long as they both had. "Live for the moment, right?"

And then he was standing before her, looking down at the face of the woman who had always held his life in her hands.

"Sounds good to me." Terrance smiled at her, feeling the ends of his own smile swirling all through him. "So, are you planning on staying overdressed like that all night?"

"That's up to you." There was a wicked glimmer in her eyes as she raised them to his.

Terrance hooked his forefinger in the rim of the towel just between her breasts and pulled her to him, then stopped. He glanced up the stairs.

"Maybe we'd better take this to your room. If Julie should wander out, I think this might be way too much of an education for her to handle."

His thoughtfulness touched her. There was so much of the old Terrance in this man who had reentered her life. "Julie's at Grandpa's tonight. He thought I needed to get my rest."

He thought of their first night together. "I do truly love that father of yours."

There was no further discussion about destination. With Julie gone there was no reason to move anywhere. The whole house was theirs.

With a quick, gentle movement of his fingers, the towel found itself communing with the floor, forming a semi-circle of white dampness on the entry tiles beneath her feet.

Drawing her to him, absorbing her warmth, he smiled. "You smell of flowers."

"That's my bubble bath."

Terrance tilted her head up and brushed his lips against hers. "And of sin."

"That would be your work." Alix entwined her arms around his neck, bringing herself up on her toes to kiss him more deeply.

Her body brushed along his, sending electric shock waves through it along with a surge of heat.

Reacting, his arms closed around Alix, locking her into place as his mouth finished what hers had begun. The kiss had the depth and breadth of an ocean, engulfing them both.

He wasn't sure if he undressed himself or if she did. Most likely it was a combination of both their efforts. All Terrance knew was that within a heartbeat, he was as naked as she was. As eager as she was to reach their own special place, the haven where the world couldn't find them. Where there were no lies, no lives that depended on him, no consequences to be faced.

There was only her, only him, only the intense feelings they had for one another.

That he loved her as much as he was capable of loving anyone he never doubted. If that was enough, he didn't know.

But for now, he didn't have to know. All he had to do was be with her. Make love with her. It was more than he would have dreamed of only a month ago.

Wrapped around each other, they sank down to the floor, and she moaned, shifting. The movement aroused him, but he was aware that the moan might have come from discomfort. He raised himself slightly. "Too hard?"

"What?"

"The floor." Raising himself further, he bracketed her body on either side with his hands. "Is it too hard for you?"

Alix laughed. "I thought maybe you were referring to yourself." The laughter tucked itself away into her grin, her eyes remaining fixed on his. She could have been lying on a bed of nails right now and she wouldn't have noticed. She slid her fingers along his face. "Will you carry me up the stairs again?"

"That depends." He cocked his head, as if studying her from this close vantage point. "Have you gained any weight since the last time?"

"Beast," she said with a sniff.

"I'll take that as a yes." And then he rose, drawing her up with him. Before she could say a word in response, she was up in his arms again. "I guess I can give it my best shot."

"As I remember," Alix curled her body against his chest, her arms around his neck, "you have a lot of best shots."

The sound of his laughter, rumbling in his chest and against her cheek, sent comforting ripples through her body. It made her feel oh, so safe, so secure. And in love, she added silently. Safe, secure and in love. At least for the moment.

He caught her lips, kissing her hard just before he began to walk up the stairs with her.

"I could get used to this," she murmured with a heartfelt sigh.

So could he, he thought. But he couldn't allow himself to. Because once Alix found out his secret, everything would change.

He wasn't saying anything, she thought. No flippant, teasing remark had met hers in response. She knew what that meant. Terrance wasn't given to lies or to making promises. Not anymore.

But that was all right, she wasn't asking for any, wasn't pretending any existed. She was an adult now, and that meant knowing that all anyone ever had was this moment in time. Nothing more, nothing less. She intended to make the most of hers.

"Is it my imagination, or are you getting slower?" she teased, determined to enjoy herself and not overthink anything.

He was relieved that the serious moment was over. "If you're going to complain—"

Pretending to take umbrage, he deposited her unceremoniously on her bed. With a whoop of surprise, Alix bounced once, her eyes flying open. The next moment she scrambled up to her knees and caught his arm, throwing him off balance and onto the bed.

Onto her.

Terrance had to brace his arms on either side of her to keep from coming down too hard. He loved the way her laughter echoed in his chest.

"If I didn't know any better, I would have said you planned that."

Alix laughed, arching her body so that it pressed into his. "I did."

The laughter died as he looked into her face, regretting the years he had lost, aching for the years he wouldn't have. Blotting out all thought, he brought his mouth down to hers.

The moment he did, the fire lit and began to consume them both in earnest.

He meant to go slowly, to take each step languidly, weaving it into the last. Memorizing the curve of her body, the tastes of her skin, everything. But the demands of passion were too hard to contain. So he made love to her as if there was no time left.

Because perhaps there wasn't.

Alix felt his hands everywhere, her mind spinning out of control as he touched her, caressed her. Pressed his palms along her body and branded her.

His lips followed almost immediately, fanning the flames. Making her crazy. Making her want him so badly, even her teeth hurt.

Terrance knew how to play her, he always had. He knew where to touch, where to arouse. It felt as if she had been transformed into one enormous climax because no sooner had he brought her to one than another began to unfold, demanding her, taking her.

Everywhere his lips touched, she felt tiny explosions. Whether it was the hollow of her neck, the dip in her elbow, the place behind her knee, the sensation happened again and again until she felt that her body had been entirely depleted of energy. Damp and panting, she sank into the mattress, convinced that she was going to fade from life in the next moment. With a smile on her face.

And then he was pushing himself into her, full and wanting, his eyes on hers. She'd never seen him like this.

A new wave of craving overtook her, energizing her, exhausting her. She didn't think she had enough strength to match the rhythm of his hips, but she was wrong. All it took was wanting to please him, wanting to be there with him when he experienced the final release that took him over the brink.

He locked his hands with hers, lacing them together, holding them down firmly against the bed.

At the very last moment he caught her lips with his own and cried out her name. She thought he said something more, but she couldn't be sure. The haze that was around her was too thick, too consuming. It took every effort for her just to be able to breathe.

After she opened her eyes, she felt almost too spent to draw her lips back in a smile. All she could manage was to turn her head ever so slightly.

"Wow."

"I'll take that as a compliment," he murmured against her neck, too exhausted for the moment to even raise his head.

Was it possible? Feeling his breath along her skin was stirring her. "Was there some kind of fire you were rushing to?"

She felt his lips curving against her neck as he smiled. Something fluttered in her stomach, twisting. "Did you feel rushed?"

She sighed. "I felt wonderful." Lifting one leaden arm, she stroked his hair. "I *feel* wonderful."

This time he did rouse himself just enough to look at her. "Yes, you do."

She could feel the sweat between their bodies, feel her hair plastered against her skin, just as his was against his. The sensation enticed her. Lifting her head a little, she pressed a kiss against the back of his head. And then she fell back. "What just happened here?"

He could feel her heart beating hard against her rib cage, echoing its erratic rhythm against his chest. With effort, he raised himself up on his elbows and looked down at her face. "If I have to explain it, then I did it wrong."

She smiled, memorizing every nuance of his face, loving everything she saw.

Love. Was that what she'd heard him say along with her name? Were the muffled words "I love you?" Or was that just wishful thinking on her part? She wasn't sure, but she wasn't going to ask and spoil it all. Better to just pretend.

As if to hide her thoughts, she laced her hands together behind his neck, drawing him closer.

"You did it perfectly," she assured him. "I just never knew you to be so intense before."

There was something in his expression, something that had haunted her before. However reluctantly, her thoughts returned to her phone call to Stephanie. Back to her questions. She would have hoped her doubts would have remained at bay just a little longer. It saddened her.

"Is there anything wrong?" she asked, searching his face for some kind of sign, some kind of clue. "You can tell me, Terry."

He took her hand and brought it to his lips, kissing her fingers one by one. It was getting harder and harder to keep things from her. "You just called me Terry again."

"Did I?" She hadn't realized that. Alix caught her lower lip between her teeth. "Maybe it's a vulnerable moment." The smile faded a little. "I don't like being vulnerable, Terry."

He knew that and hated the game he had to play. "Then trust me."

I want to. I really, really want to. But the danger was that she was risking her heart, a heart she might not be able to repair a second time. "That makes me most vulnerable of all." Alix took a deep breath, knowing there was no resolving this issue tonight.

Or perhaps any night.

She wasn't going to think about it. She couldn't. Instead she turned her body into his, her eyes gleaming mischievously. "Ready for round two?"

"You've got to be kidding." He laughed, grateful for the reprieve.

She looked at him, affecting the most solemn expression she could muster. "I never kid when I'm naked."

"I'll do my best."

She was already under him, moving to ensure his compliance, her arms woven around his neck. "That's all I ask, Terrance, that's all I ask."

She'd called him Terrance. The moment was over. But not the lovemaking, he thought, as he gave himself up to the feeling that was even now taking hold of him again. For now, that was all that counted.

The sound of a voice, low and hushed, wormed its way into her sleep and roused Alix. She'd never been a very heavy sleeper, and motherhood had all but destroyed her ability to blot out noises of any decibel level.

"Terrance?" She felt behind her. The emptiness made her turn.

The spot beside her was empty.

And still warm.

The next moment she realized that it was Terrance's voice she was hearing. It sounded as if it was coming from the hallway. Was there someone in the house?

The last haze of sleep vanished. Quickly Alix got out of bed and padded over to where her robe was slung across the back of a chair. She put it on, knotting the sash as she stepped out into the hallway. She debated calling to him.

She didn't have to. He was in the guest room. On the phone.

Terrance didn't have to be told she was in the room. He sensed it. He only prayed he'd sensed it in time and that she hadn't overheard anything.

"I'll talk to you later," he told Riley abruptly.

There was no time to explain. Terrance replaced the receiver in its cradle, breaking the connection. Turning, he gave her his most engaging smile.

"I didn't want to wake you," he said in response to the look on her face.

There was more to it than that, she sensed. But what? "Very considerate." She nodded at the small pink phone. "Who were you talking to?"

"The hospital." And then, because it made no sense for him to be calling them, he added, "They called."

Her eyes never left his face. Why are you lying to me, Terrance? "I didn't hear the phone."

He walked out of the small guest room and went back to her bedroom. Alix had no choice but to follow. "That's because they called on my pager."

Another lie. What was going on here? "You left your clothes downstairs," she pointed out. "The pager would have had to have been amplified to the level of a siren for you to hear it beeping from up here."

Why was it that he could stare anyone else in the eye and lie to them without so much as twitching an eyelash, and yet he couldn't come up with a simple cover story for himself when it came to Alix? How was it that she managed to press all of his buttons, short-circuit all his lines this way?

"Who were you calling?" She placed herself in front of him, wanting to see his eyes.

Cornered, he gave her the first name that popped into his head. "All right, if you have to know, I was talking to Harris."

She stared at him incredulously, all the stories that she'd recently heard about the doctor coming back. "Why? What earthly reason would you have for sneaking out of my bed, a bed where we'd made love, to talk to that man?"

"I told him I'd call him to make arrangements for tonight." He looked at her significantly. "I like keeping my word."

None of this was making any sense to her. "Giving your word to a snake doesn't count. Besides, I thought you said you didn't like him."

He couldn't lie and say that he did. She would see right through that one. "I don't." He could see her protest coming. "But it's complicated."

"All right, then uncomplicate it."

"I can't just yet." He slipped off the jeans he'd tugged on earlier to make the call. He wasn't wearing any underwear.

She tried not to allow the state of his body to distract her, but even worried, it wasn't easy to ignore the finest specimen of manhood she had ever seen. "Terrance, are you in debt to William or something?"

"What makes you ask that?"

"Because there's a rumor that he's into something dirty. That he owes some casino bosses a lot of money. His father doesn't know, or is turning a deaf ear to the talk, but what the Harrises do is their concern. What you do is mine." She placed an imploring hand on his arm. "Terrance, I don't want you getting mixed up in any of this. Who knows the kind of people he's connected with. You could get hurt."

He wanted to tell her, to at least partially erase the lines of worry from her forehead. He suddenly hated the restrictions of his job. They'd never bothered him before, but now they were disrupting his life.

He cupped her cheek. "You don't have to worry," he assured her. Taking her hand, he laced his fingers through it and began drawing her farther into the room. "Now come back to bed. We both don't have to be in for another hour."

She glanced at the clock on the nightstand. "I need to shower and get dressed. That doesn't leave much time," she pointed out.

His grin only became more wicked. "Let me show you what I can do under pressure."

She didn't want to be distracted, but she couldn't help it. "You could probably sell needles to cacti."

"I'm not interested in cacti. I'm interested in something far less prickly than spiny plants." He brushed a kiss to her lips. "Now come to bed, you just wasted fifteen seconds."

"I'll shower faster," she promised.

Alix slipped into bed and into his arms.

Chapter 14

Her hair still damp from the shower she'd just taken, Alix opened the refrigerator. "You can have eggs and toast or eggs and toast," she offered.

He glanced at his watch, estimating his time margin. "I'll take just toast—to go."

Taking out the loaf of bread, she was about to ask Terrance what the hurry was when the phone rang. She picked up the receiver and cradled it against her neck and shoulder as she deposited four slices of bread into the toaster.

"Hello?"

"Alix? It's Stephanie. I did a little more research into this Terrance McCall of yours."

Alix raised her eyes to look at Terrance, who was helping himself to a quick cup of coffee. "And?"

"He's in our database all right."

Alix breathed an audible sigh of relief. He hadn't lied. Guilt pricked her. She was just being overly cautious, that's all.

"Impressive list of credentials, too," Stephanie was saying. "Not to mention that he looks like a really honey. But the funny thing is, when I asked around in pediatrics, nobody seems to remember dealing with him."

Alix's fingers tightened around the telephone. Damn it, there *was* something wrong after all.

"I don't know what to make of it, Alix, but there it is."

The lead weight was back on her chest. Somehow she mustered a semicheery response. "Thanks, Stephanie. I owe you."

"If this McCall turns out to be legit, you can hook me up with his brother if he has one."

Alix murmured something to Stephanie in response, though what it was she couldn't remember even as she hung up the phone. The toast popped up behind her, but her mind was no longer on breakfast. She turned around to look at the man in her kitchen. The man she'd just made love with again.

The man she didn't know.

He didn't like the expression on her face. It was as if she was looking straight into his soul. Terrance placed his empty cup on the counter.

"What's the matter?" He tried to second-guess what she was thinking. "Another patient?"

"No, a doctor." For a moment something went dead inside her. And then anger began to bubble. "That was my friend who works at Boston General." She watched him. He was cool, she thought. He never even missed a beat. A man less given to lying for a living would have looked at least a little uncomfortable.

She hated him for hurting her all over again.

"They want me back?" he kidded.

"They might," she replied, her voice low, "if they knew who you were."

Damn it. She knew. Somehow she knew. But he was bound to continue playing the game. "What are you talking about?" His face was the soul of innocence. "I was there for four years—"

Alix could have scratched his eyes out. "Why don't you stop lying and tell me the truth, Terrance? Who the hell are you?" she demanded angrily. "Why are you here?"

His eyes fixed on hers. "I'm who I always was, Alix. And I'm here because I need to be." He took a step toward her, his hand outstretched. "Because you're here."

Alix knocked it away. "No twitches, no nose growing." There was nothing but contempt in her voice. "You've really mastered this lying thing, haven't you?"

"Alix—" For the life of him, he didn't know what to say, how to make it right.

"This has something to do with Harris, doesn't it? I don't know how, but it does. I can feel it." A sense of panic began to set in, spreading in her soul like a tipped-over bottle of black ink on a snow-white sheet of paper. "Whatever it is, back away, Terrance. Please back away before it's too late. Before Harris drags you down with him."

He tried to reach for her again, to calm her, but she moved back. She was looking at him as if she didn't know him. Terrance felt torn between duty and something greater.

"Nobody's dragging anyone down, Alix. You're just going to have to trust me for a little while longer."

She knew it. "Then there *is* something going on."

Terrance shook his head, helpless. "Alix, I can't—"

There it was, she thought. In a nutshell. Why was she even trying?

"No, you can't, can you?" She struggled to re-sign herself to the inevitable. Nothing had changed. "Can't let me in now any more than you could be-fore. I was deluding myself, hoping that I could just take this on a day-by-day basis." *Fool,* she up-braided herself. "But secretly I was praying you had come finally around. That this time it was permanent—'' She bit her lip to keep the tears back.

He saw them shimmering in her eyes. It tore him up to see her this way. He didn't know what to say.

"But it's not, is it?" she demanded, suddenly angry that he was sacrificing something wonderful for who knew what reason. Angry that she didn't matter enough for him to turn his back on whatever was going on and just trust her. Just be with her. "You're shutting me out just the way you did before. And you'll be leaving, just like you did before." She fisted her hands at her sides. "Go ahead, deny it."

His eyes held hers. "Would you believe me if I did?"

"No." For a moment the silence was deafening. And then his pager went off. She saw him look down at the number, then reach into his pocket for the cell phone he hardly even seemed to be without. Her eyes widened incredulously. How could he stop in the middle like this? "Don't answer that," she warned. "I know it's not the hospital, don't answer that."

It was Riley. He knew why his partner was paging him. The answer was positive. The shipment was coming. He had to get down there. Crossing to the doorway, he shook his head. "I have to."

Stunned, all she could do was stare at him. "Don't you dare leave. We're in the middle of an argument. If you leave, it's over, do you hear me? It's over!''

"We'll talk later, I promise." He crossed back, grabbed hold of her and kissed her, hard and quick. And then he was gone.

"There isn't going to be a later," Alix cried after him.

She heard the front door close.

Frustrated, Alix grabbed the first thing she could reach, a dish, and threw it against the wall. The tears that had been stinging her eyes began to fall.

It was going down.

He knew it. The call to Riley on his cell phone as he drove to the hospital was merely to confirm what he already knew. The laundry trucks were arriving, possibly even now, and inside information via the wiretap had tipped them off that this shipment had more than starched uniforms and freshly disinfected sheets in it. This particular shipment had six kilos of cocaine buried in the bottoms of the large laundry baskets used to transport the linens from the trucks into the hospital's basement.

The overall plan was simple. Drugs came into the country and had to be hidden until distribution was accounted for and in place. No one, the key figures contended, would expect to find them in the basement of a hospital as reputable as Blair Memorial.

When the time came, the drugs were moved out the same way they had come in, ready to hit the streets.

It was perfect.

Until someone had talked, trading the information for a get-out-of-jail-free card.

Terrance pulled up to the parking lot on the far side of the hospital, out of the way of the general population in the area where the delivery trucks made their stops.

He saw the laundry trucks.

Saw, too, that his people had converged and were getting ready.

He spotted Riley, still dressed in his orderly uniform, behind a cable truck that had supposedly been called in to fix a reception problem. He recognized it as one of theirs.

Terrance was quick to make his way over.

There were twelve of them, counting Riley and himself. Twelve DEA people to surround several baskets, Juarez, the security guard they now knew was in on it and several Brite Day Laundry transport workers who probably weren't. Terrance had no doubt that the people running the operation weren't going to take minimum-wage workers into their confidence. As a precaution everyone ordinarily involved in the Brite Day Laundry's run had been checked out for priors and history. Other than a few traffic violations sustained before they came to work for the company, the records were all clean.

But a person could never be sure.

Terrance joined Riley behind a cable truck positioned near the basement entrance. Riley smirked at his partner as he strapped a bullet-proof vest on.

"Glad you could tear yourself away from your love life and make it." Riley slid his tunic over the vest. The blue material strained at the excess bulk.

Terrance spared him a glance before looking back at the entrance. One of the baskets was being unloaded. "You look fat. When did the trucks get here?"

"I look muscular," Riley contradicted. "The trucks came minutes ago. We just saw the first one go by the surveillance camera inside the far corridor." Thanks to Monroe splicing the pickup, they could see everything that ordinary surveillance picked up in the basement. "Our sticky-fingered security guard opened the back doors for the laundry boys. Big surprise."

Terrance just wanted this part of it to be over. He craned his neck to look around the side of the cable truck again. "Harris there?"

Riley checked the weapon strapped to his ankle. He tucked the pants leg down again. "It's his neck if something goes wrong. What do you think?"

Terrance made sure his own gun was readily accessible, then rose. "I think I'd better get myself down into the basement. They want an eyewitness for this, right? I figure I'm elected."

Riley stood up beside him. "I can play hero, too."

Terrance knew it was his partner's way of looking out for him. "I've got the face for it. You can play the faithful sidekick."

"Hey, if you think I'm going to settle for being typecast at my tender age, think again." Riley grew serious. "You'll need backup closer than half a parking lot away. Harris doesn't strike me as playing with a full deck."

Terrance nodded. Riley was right. They stood a better chance of coming out alive if there were two of them going in together.

"Not even close," he agreed. Terrance shook his head as one of the men offered him a vest. The scrubs he had on were a size too small. Ironically, they had shrunken in the wash. A vest would make him too bulky and tip Juarez off. "Dead giveaway, no pun intended." He started to lead the way out, then stopped. He looked at Riley. "Look, if anything goes wrong—"

It was bad luck to talk about death just before a mission went down. Riley cut him off. "It won't."

But Terrance wanted to get this out. "Tell Alix I'm sorry."

"Okay." Riley nodded, going with the scenario. "Then she'll throw herself into my arms, sobbing. We'll comfort each other, fall in love and have six kids. The second one we'll name after you."

Laughing, Terrance hit him with the flat of his hand, urging him out. "The hell you will." He took a deep breath. "Okay, let's roll."

It was a bright, sunny day. It didn't seem like the kind of day anything dark could happen. But failure and oblivion, Terrance knew as they walked out into the open, were only a bullet away.

Alix didn't know why she cared. He obviously didn't. But Terrance was setting himself up for disaster, and she couldn't bear to see anything happen to him. Someone had to intervene.

The idiot had no one to stand up for him. If something bad happened, if whatever this was that involved Harris should come back to bite them, Harris had his father to turn to. Money could always be counted on to buy people out of dire situations.

But there would be no one for Terrance, no one to buy him out. Harris was the type to turn on anyone to save himself. She didn't know what was going on, but she'd heard rumors about gambling debts, rumors about drugs and underworld types. If Harris had somehow managed to drag Terrance into this...

She had to stick by him, at least until she could talk some sense into him. Or, she thought suddenly, as she pulled onto the hospital grounds, if not him, then maybe she could prevail on Harris.

Alix turned left toward the parking lot that was

set aside strictly for the use of physicians. Harris's red Ferrari was parked in its prime spot.

That was odd. As far as she knew, he wasn't supposed to be here until later.

Good. If he was here, she could talk to him, try to appeal to his kinder side—provided it hadn't been surgically removed yet.

Getting out, she pressed the security button on her keychain. Her vehicle softly squawked in response. She didn't relish having any interaction with the man. Since their last date, Harris had gone out of his way to be nasty to her whenever they crossed paths. He was a petulant, spoiled child, and she would rather have steered clear of him.

But this wasn't about her, it was about Terrance, damn his pigheadedness.

Alix glanced at her watch. She was early. Her rotation in the E.R. didn't begin yet. For once, none of the patients on the pediatric floor were hers. Since Harris was somewhere on the premises, that meant she could try to get this over with and talk to him.

She punched his pager number out on her cell phone. Knowing him, Harris'd probably think she was using this to come on to him. The man's ego was insufferable.

"You owe me, Terrance," she murmured under her breath, walking in through the hospital's electronic doors.

* * *

Harris jerked around nervously. His pager had just gone off, and he thought he heard footsteps coming down the basement corridor.

The heavyset man beside him laughed mockingly. The sound echoed around them.

"Be cool, man," Juarez hissed. "Nobody suspects nothin'. You're acting like some virgin at a stag party." The contempt on his face was obvious. He waved the next basket down the entrance and toward him. "Relax. Answer your pager later."

And then he heard it, too. Someone was coming.

Moving in front of Harris, Juarez walked up to the two men who had just turned down the hall. He recognized the taller of the two.

"I think you took a wrong turn, Doctor." Juarez deliberately ignored the orderly beside the physician, regarding him as someone beneath his own position. "This is laundry day. There's nothing down here on this side but the laundry." Juarez pointed down the corridor from which Terrance had come. "The cafeteria's in the opposite direction."

Terrance glanced over his shoulder. "Guess I kind of got turned around. But this is lucky." He gestured at the basket that had just been brought in. "Because as it happens, I need some dry clothes." Terrance began to move around Juarez.

The latter deliberately put his body in between Terrance and the basket. Dark, threatening eyes swept over him. "You look pretty dry to me, Doc."

Terrance looked down at himself, as if confused, then brightened as he looked up. It was a game of cat and mouse now. "It's not for me. Dr. Graywolf had a patient throw up on him." Again, he moved past Juarez. Behind the security guard, he could see Harris looking at them, a deer caught in the head-lights of an oncoming truck. "I said I'd come down and get him a change of clothes. The smell's aw-ful."

"These are just linens and towels," Juarez in-formed him. The jovial note was forced. "Uniforms are already in the closets. Why don't you try—"

But Terrance hadn't budged. "You sure?" He looked down into the basket, moving aside the piles.

"You're messing things up, Doc," Juarez warned. His hand went to his gun. The message was clear.

Harris came to life. "Take it easy, Juarez." He licked his lips nervously, looking from one man to the other. "It's only McCall, my drinking buddy, right?" He looked at Terrance hopefully. "Fresh uniforms have already been taken upstairs, like he said, McCall."

Harris was set to go off at any second, Terrance thought. He didn't have to look behind him to know that Riley was ready.

"You know a lot about laundry for a doctor, Har-ris," he said easily. Terrance suddenly pulled back a pile of sheets. Small plastic packages of white

powder were neatly nestled below. "What's that?"
Terrance raised his eyes to Juarez. "Talcum powder?"

Juarez didn't wait any longer to pull his security
gun and aimed it at Terrance. There was sweat on
his upper lip. "I told you to back off, Doc. Now
you've made things complicated."

Harris hadn't bargained on anyone getting hurt.
Afraid, he attempted to intervene. "I told you, he's
all right."

Juarez suddenly made a connection. "You told
him?" he cried. With a quick motion, he turned and
aimed his gun at Harris. "You freakin' bastard! You
sold us out!"

"No, no, I'd never do that!" Harris cried like a
stuck pig.

The shot meant for Harris went wild as Riley
grabbed his arm, pushing it upward.

Yelping like a wounded, frightened animal, Harris pushed the wagon into the other three men and
ran into the bowels of the hospital.

Springing to his feet first, Juarez released a bar-
rage of foul language as he fired at Riley. Terrance
dove into his partner, knocking him out of the way,
but it was too late. Hit, Riley went down.

"You son of a bitch!" Terrance shouted, shooting at Juarez's knee. The latter screamed and went
down, his gun flying out of his hand as he clutched
his knee.

The men just entering the basement quickly scattered, letting go of the basket they'd been pushing. Picking up speed, it came crashing down on Juarez, laundry mingling with white plastic packages. Terrance knew that the DEA posted outside would quickly converge on the fleeing workers.

His weapon trained on Juarez, Terrance called for backup as he hurried to Riley.

"Officer down, officer down. Seal off all the exits." He dropped to his knees beside his partner. The latter was pale and still, his eyes closed.

Like a delayed echo, it suddenly occurred to Terrance that there was no blood. He shook Riley's shoulder, trying to get him to come around.

"How bad is it?"

Opening his eyes, Riley groaned, trying to catch his breath.

"Like a mule just kicked me in the chest," he said weakly. Riley felt around the area, amazed at the pain. More amazed to be alive. "They don't tell you about that part."

Wanting to assure himself, Terrance ripped open his partner's shirt. The three bullets had sunken into his vest. Terrance blew out a breath of relief. "Damn, I could kiss you."

Groggily drawing himself up into a sitting position, Riley laughed, pushing his partner back. "Save it for your girlfriend."

Alix.

Harris was still loose. There was no telling what the man was capable of, now that everything was coming down on him. Terrance was on his feet instantly. "You okay to leave alone?"

Riley already had his spare weapon in his hand, the muzzle aimed at Juarez, who was cursing at them and bleeding badly. "I've been on dates before, McCall, no need to chaperone me. Go after Harris."

Terrance was already running down the corridor. Harris had a two-minute start on him. There was a sinking feeling in his chest—Harris was completely unpredictable, a loose cannon. There was no telling what he would do next, now that he thought he was going to be sent to prison.

Impatience ate away at Alix as she left the doctor's lounge. Harris wasn't there. She'd paged him, but had gotten no response. Time was getting short. Her shift in the E.R. began in a few minutes. It looked as if she was going to have to delay talking to Harris until later.

Maybe in that time, the problem—whatever it was—would resolve itself. But she doubted it.

Just as she turned a corner, she saw the fire door leading to the stairs fly open. Harris came rushing out. Even from this distance, he looked crazed, frightened.

Alix's first thought was of Terrance. Had something happened to him? She ran toward Harris.

"William, what's wrong?" she called out.

He spun around, looking for all the world like prey searching for somewhere to hide. Recognition came after a beat. The uneasiness she felt gave way to concern.

"Are you all right?" she asked as she reached him.

Instead of answering her, he grabbed her arm, twisting it behind her back as he yanked her to him.

His fevered brain desperately tried to think of a course of action. A hostage, he needed a hostage. If he had someone, they couldn't shoot him.

She tried to twist out of his grasp, but he yanked harder. Pain shot up her arm. "William, what the hell are you doing?"

"Shut up," he cried, his voice cracking with fear. "You're going to get me out of here."

Seeing a door, he pushed his way in. It was an out-patient lab, one of two located on the first floor. Several people sat in the chairs that lined the walls. A daytime talk-show host droned on, on the television screen just above their heads.

The instant Harris burst in, dragging Alix with him, the atmosphere changed to one of fear.

"Everybody out!" he screamed, waving his hand to the door.

It was then that she realized he was holding a gun.

Chapter 15

Harris tightened his fingers around the gun he'd picked up just before he'd run down the corridor— the gun that had flown out of the orderly's hand when Juarez had shot him. Except the man hadn't been an orderly, he'd been a cop. Like that scum McCall was a cop.

Harris felt hysteria building within him.

Nobody was who they were supposed to be anymore.

"I said, get out!" he screamed, waving his gun menacingly at the cowering patients.

It was as if a dam had broken. Frightened, the patients scrambled for the door, pushing their way into the corridor.

Alix clenched her teeth to keep from crying out from the pain in her arm and shoulder. "William, what is going on here?" she demanded. "Why are you waving that gun around?"

There was pounding in his head, making it hard to think. He'd come in, hungover and afraid, in no condition to handle what was going down. He lived in fear of these people he was forced to deal with. And then, just when it looked as if it was going to be all right, all hell had broken loose.

He couldn't make any sense of his thoughts.

"Shut up. Shut up!" he ordered, his voice nearly breaking. "I have to think." His eyes darted back and forth in the room, making sure there wasn't someone lying in wait for him, waiting to bring him down.

He jumped when the phone inside the lab rang.

Harris pushed Alix around to the back of the desk. "Answer it!"

Alix picked up the receiver with both hands, her eyes never leaving the gun that Harris was brandishing nervously. In his condition the weapon could go off at any moment.

"Hello?" She heard a woman's voice on the other end, asking about the lab's hours. Her mind went blank. "The lab is closed right now. Call back later."

Alix dropped the receiver into the cradle, only to have the phone ring again the second it made contact. Damn it, didn't the woman understand English?

Her throat dry, Alix yanked up the receiver again. "I'm sorry, but—" She stopped as she heard the voice on the other end. She could have cried. "Terrance? Terrance, what's going on here? Why is William waving a gun at me? What's happening?"

The people fleeing the laboratory, shouting something about a terrorist invasion, had run straight for the front of the hospital. And right past Terrance. He had caught one of them, a terrified woman of about forty, and asked her what was going on. She'd told him that a man with a gun had dragged a woman into the lab and then thrown them all out. When he asked if the man had on a lab coat, she'd said yes. Harris.

His gut had told him that Alix was the woman taken hostage.

Terrance had had the switchboard put him through to the lab. "Don't panic, Alix, we'll get you out of there."

Nerves clawed at her. She struggled not to give way. "Talk to me," she demanded. "What the hell is going on here?"

Harris grabbed the receiver away from her, motioning her back with his gun. "That's enough. I'm in charge," he informed Terrance.

"You're the man with the gun," Terrance replied, his voice level and calming. "Let me come in, Harris. I'll be your hostage. Let Alix go. A DEA agent is more valuable to them than a doctor.''

Harris shifted from foot to foot, indecision gnawing at him. Then he thought of the rumors he'd heard about Alix and McCall. ''No. As long as I have her, you'll do what I want.''

You hurt her, I'll kill you with my bare hands. It wasn't easy for Terrance to keep his voice calm. ''It's not up to me, Harris.''

''*Make it* up to you.''

He had to get inside the room. ''Only chance I have is to come inside to talk. Otherwise, I can't promise anything.''

Harris rocked nervously back and forth on the balls of his feet. He wanted a drink. He wanted some of the shipment that had just come in. Most of all he wanted to be somewhere else where nothing could pressure him like this. ''All right, all right, you can come in. But leave your gun outside.''

Terrance kept his sigh of relief in check. ''Whatever you say.''

Standing before the glass door, Terrance made a show of placing his weapon on the floor in front of him. He straightened, then began walking toward the lab, his hands raised.

Harris watched, a sense of power seeping into him. He still held Alix in front of him, his hands tangled in her hair now, to keep her from moving.

But even as he waited, his gun was shaking as he held it on Terrance.

The moment the door opened, Harris took several steps back, dragging Alix with him. The small sound of pain that escaped her was involuntary.

Terrance had to contain himself not to leap for the man's throat. He couldn't take a chance on the gun going off and hurting Alix. He talked to the other man the way he would to a misguided child.

"You don't want to do this, Harris."

The rage was immediate, filling his eyes, his body, his voice. "How would you know? How would you know what I want to do?" Harris waved the gun at a nebulous audience beyond the door. "How would any of you know anything about me? Do you have any idea what it's like, never being good enough? Of always being measured by what your father and your grandfather did before you were even born?" His voice cracked before it descended into mimicry. "'You're a disgrace, William.' 'Why can't you do anything right, William?' 'You're such a disappointment, William.'" He was seething now as he remembered so many slights he'd been forced to endure. "According to them, I haven't been able to do a thing right from the day I was born!" he shouted. And then his voice dissolved into a whimper. "Nobody has ever, ever let me live my life the way I want to."

Terrance had to keep Harris talking, to distract

him until he could get hold of his gun. His hands still raised, Terrance slowly inched closer.

"Nobody told you to gamble your money away and get into debt with loan sharks and drug lords. Put the gun down, Harris. Please. I can help you. There're DEA agents all around the hospital." He could feel Alix staring at him. "Don't make this any worse than it is."

His words only seemed to enrage Harris. "You bastard!" he sobbed.

Alix stiffened. Harris was going to shoot Terrance, she could feel it. The moment he moved, she grabbed his hand, pushing it with all her might.

"No!" she screamed, throwing all her weight against him.

The bullet went into the ceiling at the same time she felt her hair being ripped out by the roots. She screamed again, this time in sheer pain.

The next thing she knew, Terrance had shot Harris in the shoulder with a weapon that hadn't been there a moment ago. The man went down, she fell on top, her hair still tangled up in his hand.

And then Terrance was beside her, freeing her from Harris's grasp. His hands on her shoulders, he brought her up to her feet. "Are you all right?"

Tears of pain were in her eyes. Getting hold of herself, she nodded.

"I'm fine," she breathed, her heart pounding.

But she wasn't.

Not yet, not until she knew what was going on.

The next moment the room was alive with people she didn't recognize, crowding into the room, all talking at once. Men with body armor and helmets. And assault rifles.

She looked at Terrance. He looked vastly underdressed in comparison.

And he had been the one to come in first.

To save her.

She realized she was shaking, and hugged herself to try to stop.

"Take him down to the office," Terrance was ordering a man who came in behind him. Then he turned to Alix, his face lined with concern. He ran his hands up and down her arms to assure himself that there were no overlooked wounds. There were no damp stains forming, no wetness to bear witness to any blood flowing.

He looked into her face. If anything had happened to her...

"Are you sure you're all right?"

Numbly she nodded, watching as Harris was led off in handcuffs, sobbing.

Alix stood back out of the way, as more and more people came into the small room. They were gathering around Terrance, saying things, asking questions, waiting for orders.

He looked like a field general, not a doctor.

His last set of instructions fading in the air, Terrance looked over his shoulder at Alix. He couldn't fathom the expression on her face. It wasn't shock. He'd seen shock before and this wasn't it.

It was distance, he realized. That was what was on her face. Distance. The kind of unfathomable distance that occurred between a man and a woman when there was no middle ground.

"McCall—"

Terrance waved back the man, hardly sparing him a look. The bust had gone down, and he needed to put his life together.

"Give us a minute. Wait for me outside," he instructed his subordinate. With that, he ushered out the last of them and then turned back to Alix. Waiting.

She looked at him as if she'd never seen him before. Because maybe she hadn't. "So this was what you couldn't tell me." Her voice was dead, emotionless. "You're not a doctor."

It wasn't strictly true. He had his degree. But they weren't nit-picking here.

"Not a practicing one, no." He tried to head off what he knew was coming. "I couldn't tell you who I was or what I was doing because there were lives at stake."

She stared at him incredulously. What had been going through his head? "And you thought, what? That I'd sell the story to a tabloid? That I'd go running to Harris and tell him everything in exchange for the honor of becoming his gun moll?''

She made it sound ridiculous, but there had been legitimate reasons behind his actions. ''I couldn't take a chance that you might let something slip.''

She laced her hands together and stared down at them. ''And risk your life.''

He would have gladly put his own life in her hands. But he hadn't the right to do that with anyone else. ''It was other lives I was worried about.''

Her head shot up. Did he think so little of her? He could have no idea how much that hurt.

''I would never, ever do anything to put lives at risk.'' She blew out a shaky breath. ''But I guess you don't know that because you don't know me. Don't trust me.''

He tried to reach for her. ''Alix—''

She jerked away. She couldn't bare to have him touch her right now. ''I think you'd better go now, Agent McCall or whatever it is you call yourself.'' She waved her hand in the air, frustrated and lacking words. ''You've got prisoners to book or tie up.''

''We—''

The look she gave him was dismissive. ''I really don't care.''

With that, she turned away and walked out the door. Ignoring questions that rose up around her, ignoring the people who attempted to swarm about her, she walked quickly toward the E.R. Toward her job and what she knew and understood.

Terrance watched her go, fighting the inclination to go after her.

But she was right, there was a job to do, and he had to attend to it. Besides, he had a feeling that she would rather see his head on a platter than talk to him right now.

She tried to bury herself in her work. That night she tried to distract herself by playing games with Julie. But her mind kept straying, wouldn't focus. Julie took her to task several times for drifting off as only a precocious two-year-old could.

She'd finally given up, bathed her daughter and put her to bed. She continued reading to her long after Julie had fallen asleep.

Nothing helped.

She just had to face up to it. There was no place in the universe for her tonight or tomorrow or the day after that. But eventually, she promised herself fiercely, it would get better.

It had to, because she didn't think it could get much worse.

When the doorbell rang, she fairly ran to it, desperate for something to distract her. If it was a salesman, she was prepared to buy every one of his subscriptions. As long as he would stay for a while and talk.

But when she opened the door, it wasn't a salesman. It was Terrance.

She raised her chin defiantly, her eyes narrowing. "What are you doing here?"

Not waiting for an invitation, he walked in. "We have to talk." He'd wrestled with his thoughts all afternoon and they had all just kept on returning to her.

She closed the door, vacillating between wanting to throw herself into his arms and wanted to beat on him. "More lies?"

"No—" he looked at her pointedly "—the truth."

She couldn't help the sarcastic remark that rose to her lips. "Sure you can trust me with it?"

He wouldn't be baited. "The operation's over. Harris couldn't wait to talk and name names in exchange for a deal."

Curiosity got the better of her. "What kind of deal?"

He recounted some of the details, the rest still had to be worked out. "Time served in a facility away from the general population. And keeping the hospital's name out of the newspapers." The latter request had surprised him, given Harris's self-centered bent.

She'd been worried about the repercussions the scandal would have within the medical community. She'd already heard of some physicians considering withdrawing their name from Blair's roster. She hadn't thought suppression was within the realm of possibilities.

"You can do that?"

He nodded. "I've got some connections, some favors to call in. Blair Memorial's name will be kept out of it."

She dragged her hand through her hair, wondering if he could make good on the promise. "Arthur Harris will be grateful."

Terrance and his superior had already met with the chairman of the board, laying the case down before him, as much as they were able. The senior Harris had held himself with a dignity that his son lacked. There were no aspirations, no threats.

"He's resigning from the board." He smiled, thinking of the man's successor. "Looks like Dr. Beauchamp'll be stepping up in the world."

He was the likely man for the job. "That leaves the chief of staff's position open," she said absently, then looked at Terrance, renewed interest in her eyes. "So what were they doing, running drugs through the hospital?"

Even as she said it, it sounded completely preposterous, like something that was scripted into a movie of the week.

He nodded. The incredible was the norm in his line of work. "Bringing in shipments in laundry baskets and keeping them on ice so to speak until the heat was off and they could be put out on the street.''

Restless, Alix moved about the room as she asked questions…keeping space between them, because she didn't trust herself not to act the part of a fool. ''How did Harris get involved?''

He told her exactly what they had learned when they went in. ''He ran up gambling debts at one of the casinos until he was drowning in them. One of the owners gave him a chance to wipe the slate clean by opening up the hospital to the trade. Harris had no choice.''

She couldn't accept that as an excuse. There was such a thing as self-respect, as honor. And Harris had not only himself to think about, but his family, his medical community. ''He *always* had a choice.''

She was careful to keep distance between them, Terrance noted. It represented the chasm that existed between them. A chasm that could only be breached one way.

''I'll quit.''

She looked up at him in surprise. She couldn't have heard him right. ''What did you say?''

He rephrased it. ''I'll leave the agency.''

Alix stared at him as the import of his words sank in. ''For me.''

''For you.''

She looked down at her nails, not seeing them as

she examined this latest bit of information he had just dropped in her lap.

"I guess I can't ask for more than that." She paused, then looked up at him. "So, I won't."

He didn't quite follow her. "You don't want me to quit," he said slowly.

"No, I don't. It's what you like to do," she explained. To ask him to give up what he did for a living just to please her would be selfish on her part, even though she knew that she was going to be worried about him for the rest of her life.

He interpreted her words the only way he could. She didn't want him in her life. He'd lost her. But he couldn't bring himself to walk away. There had to be something he could do. Because he didn't want to face the rest of his life without her.

"So, where does that leave us?"

"I don't know." She pretended to think. "The doctor and the DEA agent?"

The darkened tunnel received its first glimmer of light. He studied her face, searching for answers. Wanting to be sure he wasn't hearing what wasn't being said. "And you're okay with that?"

She stopped moving around the room and crossed to him. For the first time since he'd walked out on her this morning, she felt hopeful.

She felt like smiling.

"As long as I'm the doctor and you're the DEA agent, yes."

He'd spent the last few hours in hell, agonizing over what he would say if she turned him down. All wasted time. Thank God. But he felt it only fair to warn her. "It's not going to be easy."

She laughed. There would be evenings she wouldn't go to sleep, worrying about him. Glad to have him to worry about. "Tell me about it. The only comfort I have is that if you get shot on the job, you'll be able to operate on yourself."

He drew her into his arms. "I'd rather my wife did that."

She was definitely due for a hearing check, she decided. It sounded like he'd just said— "Wife?"

"Well, yes." Why did she looked so surprised? "What did you think I was talking about just now when I said it wasn't going to be easy?"

"That it wasn't going to be easy," she echoed. Was he pulling her leg? She'd kill him if he was. "How am I supposed to make the leap from 'easy' to 'marriage'?"

His grin was wide. "With both feet, the same as me, Alix."

She wanted this perfectly clear. "So you're asking me to marry you?"

"Asking, begging, pleading, take your pick." He brushed a kiss against her hair. She was so precious to him. He hadn't realized just how much until this morning. "I love you, Alix, and I can't see myself without you anymore."

She was still trying to take all this in. "And you were willing to give up your job for me?"

"My job, my life, whatever it takes."

Her eyes were sparkling. "You'll definitely need your life for what I have in mind."

His arms tightened around her. "So you're saying yes?"

"I've always said yes." On her toes, she nipped at his lower lip, teasing him. "Don't forget, I never said goodbye."

"Come to think of it, neither did I."

"No." She smiled for a second, before he kissed her. "You didn't."

* * * * *

If you enjoyed
UNDERCOVER M.D.,
you'll love Marie Ferrarella's exciting
new four-book miniseries:
THE MOM SQUAD.
The first book will be
available in March 2003 from
Silhouette Special Edition:
A BILLIONAIRE AND A BABY
Don't miss it!

INTIMATE MOMENTS™

presents:

Romancing the Crown

With the help of their powerful allies, the royal family of Montebello is determined to restore their heir to the throne. But their quest is not without danger—or passion!

Available in December 2002, the exciting conclusion to this year of royal romance: THE PRINCE'S WEDDING by Justine Davis (IM #1190)

When Prince Lucas Sebastiani discovered he was a father, he was determined to reunite his royal family. But would new mother Jessica Chambers accept the prince's proposal without a word of love?

This exciting series continues throughout the year with these fabulous titles:

Available only from Silhouette Intimate Moments at your favorite retail outlet.

Silhouette®

Where love comes alive™

Visit Silhouette at www.eHarlequin.com

SIMRC12

Silhouette

SPECIAL EDITION™

From *USA TODAY* bestselling author

SHERRYL WOODS

comes the continuation of the heartwarming series

The DEVANEYS

Coming in January 2003
MICHAEL'S DISCOVERY
Silhouette Special Edition #1513

An injury received in the line of duty left ex-navy SEAL
Michael Devaney bitter and withdrawn. But Michael hadn't
counted on beautiful physical therapist Kelly Andrews's healing
powers. Kelly's gentle touch mended his wounds, warmed
his heart and rekindled his belief in the power of love.

Look for more Devaneys coming in July and August 2003,
only from Silhouette Special Edition.

Available at your favorite retail outlet.

Silhouette®

Where love comes alive™

Visit Silhouette at www.eHarlequin.com   SSEMD

eHARLEQUIN.com

| | community | membership |
| buy books | authors | online reads | magazine | learn to write |

Visit eHarlequin.com to discover your one-stop
shop for romance:

buy books

♥ Choose from an extensive selection of Harlequin,
Silhouette, MIRA and Steeple Hill books.

♥ Enjoy top Silhouette authors and *New York Times*
bestselling authors in Other Romances: Nora Roberts,
Jayne Ann Krentz, Danielle Steel and more!

♥ Check out our deal-of-the-week specially discounted
books at up to 30% off!

♥ Save in our Bargain Outlet: hard-to-find books at great
prices! Get 35% off your favorite books!

♥ Take advantage of our low-cost flat-rate shipping
on all the books you want.

♥ Learn how to get FREE Internet-exclusive books.

♥ In our Authors area find the currently available titles of
all the best writers.

♥ Get a sneak peek at the great reads for the next
three months.

♥ Post your personal book recommendation online!

♥ Keep up with all your favorite miniseries.

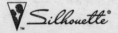

Silhouette®

where love comes alive™—online...

Visit us at
www.eHarlequin.com

SINTBB

If you enjoyed what you just read,
then we've got an offer you can't resist!

Take 2 bestselling love stories FREE!

Plus get a FREE surprise gift!

Clip this page and mail it to Silhouette Reader Service™

IN U.S.A.
3010 Walden Ave.
P.O. Box 1867
Buffalo, N.Y. 14240-1867

IN CANADA
P.O. Box 609
Fort Erie, Ontario
L2A 5X3

YES! Please send me 2 free Silhouette Intimate Moments® novels and my free surprise gift. After receiving them, if I don't wish to receive anymore, I can return the shipping statement marked cancel. If I don't cancel, I will receive 6 brand-new novels every month, before they're available in stores! In the U.S.A., bill me at the bargain price of $3.99 plus 25¢ shipping and handling per book and applicable sales tax, if any*. In Canada, bill me at the bargain price of $4.74 plus 25¢ shipping and handling per book and applicable taxes**. That's the complete price and a savings of at least 10% off the cover prices—what a great deal! I understand that accepting the 2 free books and gift places me under no obligation ever to buy any books. I can always return a shipment and cancel at any time. Even if I never buy another book from Silhouette, the 2 free books and gift are mine to keep forever.

245 SDN DNUV
345 SDN DNUW

Name	(PLEASE PRINT)	
Address	Apt.#	
City	State/Prov.	Zip/Postal Code

* Terms and prices subject to change without notice. Sales tax applicable in N.Y.
** Canadian residents will be charged applicable provincial taxes and GST.
 All orders subject to approval. Offer limited to one per household and not valid to
 current Silhouette Intimate Moments® subscribers.
 ® are registered trademarks of Harlequin Books S.A., used under license.

INMOM02   ©1998 Harlequin Enterprises Limited

$ Saving Money $
Has Never Been
This Easy!

Just fill out and send in this form from any October, November and December 2002 books and we will send you a coupon booklet worth a total savings of $20.00 off future purchases of Harlequin and Silhouette books in 2003.

Yes! It's that easy!

**I accept your incredible offer!
Please send me a coupon booklet:**

Name (PLEASE PRINT)

Address   Apt. #

City   State/Prov.   Zip/Postal Code

**In a typical month, how many
Harlequin and Silhouette novels do you read?**

❏ 0-2   ❏ 3+

097KJKDNC7   097KJKDNDP

Please send this form to:
In the U.S.: Harlequin Books, P.O. Box 9071, Buffalo, NY 14269-9071
In Canada: Harlequin Books, P.O. Box 609, Fort Erie, Ontario L2A 5X3

Allow 4-6 weeks for delivery. Limit one coupon booklet per household. Must be postmarked no later than January 15, 2003.

HARLEQUIN®
Makes any time special ®

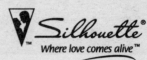

Silhouette
Where love comes alive™

© 2002 Harlequin Enterprises Limited   PHQ402

New York Times bestselling author

DEBBIE MACOMBER

weaves emotional tales of love and longing.

Here is the first
of her celebrated
NAVY series!

NAVY *Wife*

Dare Lindy risk her heart
on a man whose duty
would keep taking
him away from her?

*Available this February
wherever Silhouette books
are sold.*

Silhouette®

Where love comes alive™

Visit Silhouette at www.eHarlequin.com

PSNW

COMING NEXT MONTH

#1195 WHAT A MAN'S GOTTA DO—Karen Templeton
Single mom Mala Koleski wasn't looking for a husband—especially one like Eddie King, the sexy bad-boy-next-door she'd grown up with. When he blew back into town, alluring as ever, she swore nothing would come of their fun-filled flirtation. But was this no-strings-attached former rebel about to sign up as a family man?

#1196 ALIAS SMITH AND JONES—Kylie Brant
The Tremaine Tradition
To find her missing brother, Analiese Tremaine became Ann Smith and traveled to the South Pacific, where he'd last been seen. Her only assistance came from a mysterious man who went by the name Jones. As they searched the jungle, their passion grew hotter than the island nights. And though they had to keep their identities secret, their attraction was impossible to hide!

#1197 ALL A MAN CAN ASK—Virginia Kantra
Trouble in Eden
Hotshot Chicago detective Aleksy Denko tracked his suspect to Eden, Illinois, where a convenient cabin made the perfect base—except for stubborn, fragile Faye Harper, who refused to leave. To preserve his cover, Aleksy found himself playing house with the shy art teacher—and liking it. Until his suspect cornered Faye. Then Aleksy realized he could handle danger, but how could he handle life without Faye?

#1198 UNDER SIEGE—Catherine Mann
Wingmen Warriors
He only meant to pay a courtesy call to military widow Julia Sinclair after her son's birth, but Lt. Col. Zach Dawson ended up making an unconventional proposal. A single father wary of women, Zach asked Julia to be his wife for one year. Soon their false marriage led to real emotions and had Zach wondering what it would take to win Julia's love for life.

#1199 A KISS IN THE DARK—Jenna Mills
Falsely accused of murder, Bethany St. Croix had one chance to save herself and her unborn child: Dylan St. Croix, her ex-husband's cousin. They had shared a powerful love but now were divided by painful differences. Drawn together again, could they put their past aside in time to save their future?

#1200 NORTHERN EXPOSURE—Debra Lee Brown
Searching for a new life, fashion photographer Wendy Walters fled the city streets for the Alaskan wilderness. There she met Joe Peterson, a rugged game warden set on keeping her off his land and out of his heart. But when Wendy was targeted by an assassin, Joe rushed to her rescue, and suddenly the heat burning between them was hot enough to melt any ice.

SIMCNM1202